Also by Julie B. Cosgrove

Wordplay Mysteries

Word Has It
Word Gets Around
In Other Words
Hang On Every Word
Away With Words (coming soon)

Relatively Seeking Mysteries

One Leaf Too Many
Fallen Leaf
Leaf Me Alone

Bunco Biddies Series

Dumpster Dicing
Baby Bunco
Threes, Sixes & Thieves
'Til Dice Do Us Part

HANG ON EVERY

W O R D

by

JULIE B. COSGROVE

P

Write Integrity Press, LLC

Hang on Every Word
© 2022 Julie B Cosgrove

ISBN: 978-1-951602-13-0

Scripture references are taken from The New International Version ®NIV ®. Copyright © 1973, 1978, 1984, 2011 by Biblica, Inc. ™ Used by permission of Zondervan. All rights reserved worldwide. www.zondervan.com.

Published by Pursued Books:
an imprint of Write Integrity Press, LLC
PO Box 702852
Dallas, TX 75370

Find out more about the author, Julie B Cosgrove,
at her website: www.juliebcosgrove.com
or on her author page at www.WriteIntegrity.com.

Printed in the United States of America.

Dedication

Dedicated to my son, James who hangs on my every word. Well, sometimes.

I love you regardless and cherish our relationship.

Contents

CAST OF CHARACTERS

Wanda Lee Warner – A widow who loves word games. She has lived in Scrub Oak, TX, most of her life. She has a natural curiosity about events in her town because she loves her community and its residents. She has a dachshund named Sophie.

Betty Sue Simpson – Wanda's best friend since they were kids. She is also a widow. As a retired elementary school teacher, she knows the background of almost everyone who has lived in town since 1965. She also likes word games and puzzles.

Evelyn Joseph – Wanda's next-door neighbor who moved to Scrub Oak ten years ago to care for her sister until she passed from cancer. The widow of an Army Intelligence officer, who was killed in the Gulf War in 1990, she never remarried. She stayed in Scrub Oak because she and Wanda became good friends and she wanted to finally put down roots.

Todd Martin – Wanda's nephew, who has returned to Scrub Oak to join the police force. They have always been close and enjoy a good game of Scrabble together on Thursday mornings before his shift. He lived with Wanda during his high school years after his parents divorced.

Hazel Perks – A neighbor who lives near the old, abandoned Ferguson Mansion and is an avid gardener, which also keeps her aware of the goings on in her neighborhood. She grows prize roses.

Mayor Arnold Porter – Has been the mayor of Scrub Oak for over twenty years. He is rather pompous about his power, but deep down has the community's best interests at heart.

Chief Brooks – The police chief of Scrub Oak. All business and a stickler for rules, but underneath he has a soft heart.

Fred Ballinger – The retired principal of Scrub Oak's lower school. He has eyes for Betty Sue.

Ray O'Malley – Owner of the Hook & Owl Irish Pub, which also makes great Irish stew, Evelyn's favorite.

Jimmy Bob Arnold – The other veteran policeman in Scrub Oak.

Reagan Weber – The dispatcher and new cadet at the Scrub Oak PD.

Tom Jacobs – Owner of Tom's Thrift Shop and local editor for the *Oakmont County Weekly Gazette*. His wife is **Misty Jacobs.** His grown daughter is **Vicki Jacobs Clyburn.**

Mason Clyburn – Vicki's husband who has a business degree and a second degree in journalism. He is taking over at *The Oakmont County Weekly Gazette.*

Collin and Claudia Rollins – Runs A Cut Above, a barber/beauty salon that plays only contemporary Christian songs. Collin is a neighborhood watch captain.

Rebecca Epson – Once a cheerleader Todd crushed on in high school, she has reentered his life through Vicki and is housesitting for the Rollins.

Gail Longoria – She has opened the Bird's Nest, a pet store that promotes wildlife conservation, especially for our feathered friends.

DiAne Gates – An old college friend, now widowed, who lives in another small Texas town an hour away. Wanda talks her into coming for a visit during her church's May Fest.

Pat Farmer – The new manager of the Ferguson Mansion B&B who has organized tours as well and brought a lot of visitors to Scrub Oaks.

Micky Lozano – The head coach for the Scrub Oak High School. The baseball team is in the finals because of his efforts.

Beverly Newby – Owner of Anna's Antiques, named after her grandmother.

Anne Graves — Owner of a new restaurant Good Gravy featuring succulent roast beef and upscale comfort foods with a gourmet twist.

Henry Hampton – Owner of Hardware Haven. Always has a smile for whoever enters.

Scrub Oak, Texas

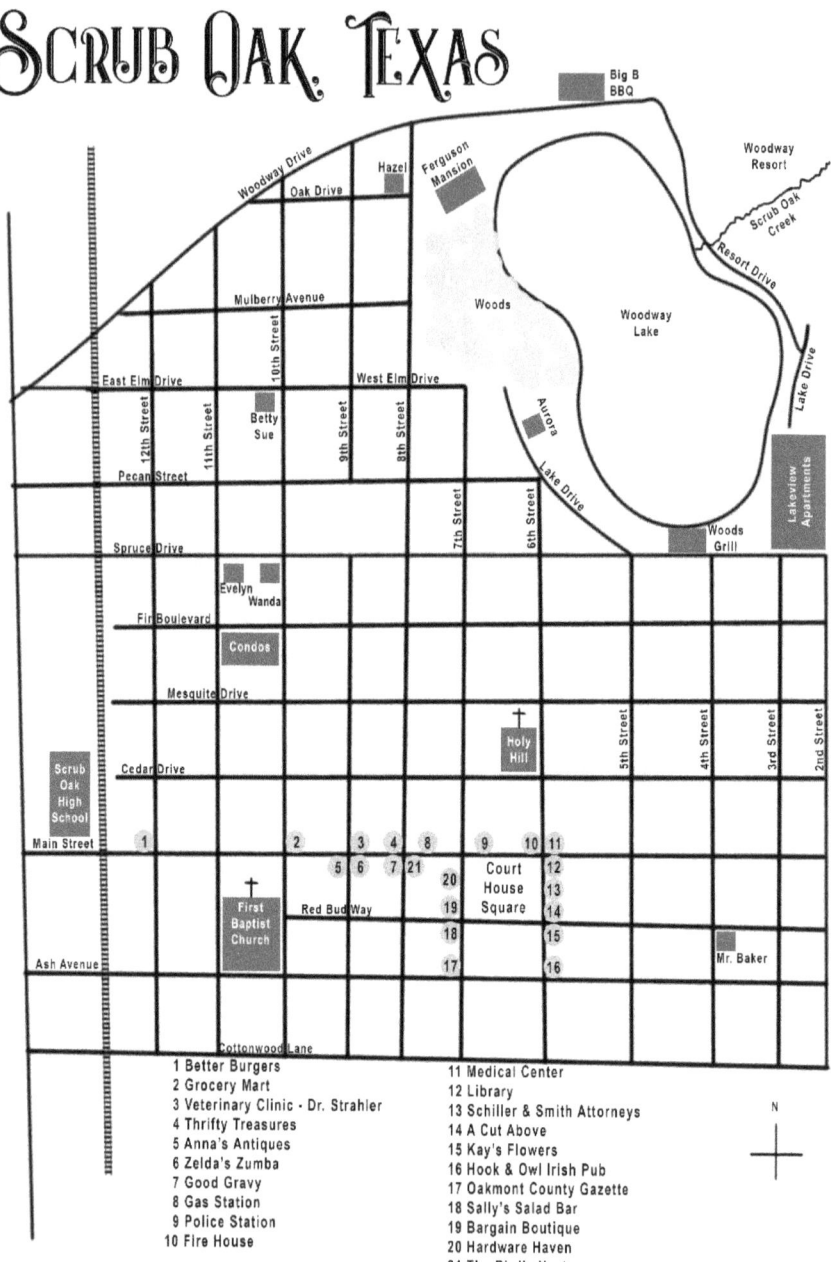

1 Better Burgers
2 Grocery Mart
3 Veterinary Clinic - Dr. Strahler
4 Thrifty Treasures
5 Anna's Antiques
6 Zelda's Zumba
7 Good Gravy
8 Gas Station
9 Police Station
10 Fire House

11 Medical Center
12 Library
13 Schiller & Smith Attorneys
14 A Cut Above
15 Kay's Flowers
16 Hook & Owl Irish Pub
17 Oakmont County Gazette
18 Sally's Salad Bar
19 Bargain Boutique
20 Hardware Haven
21 The Bird's Nest

*Anger is cruel
and fury overwhelming,
but who can stand
before jealousy?*
Proverbs 27:4

Julie B Cosgrove

CHAPTER I

Uncertainty tumbled in Wanda Warner's gut like tennis shoes in a dryer. She pressed her hand to her waist and sucked in a long breath. Why should she be nervous?

She'd been asked to meet with Tom Jacobs, editor in chief of *The Oakmont County Weekly Gazette*—not the governor of Texas for heaven's sake. She knew Tom, and in fact, had been instrumental in saving his life. But that happened a while ago. What could he possibly want now that he couldn't say over the phone?

She clucked her teeth at her silliness and smoothed her skirt. Tucking a stray strand of chestnut hair behind her ear, she noticed a few more gray shimmers. Oh, well. Tom knew her age. She'd earned every one of these silver threads, half of them in the past two years since she formed the neighborhood watches and began to help her police officer nephew, Todd, solve crimes in Scrub Oak.

Two of her peers sported a full head of grayish-white hair now, Evelyn and Hazel. That fact reminded her of what Hazel had told her just the other day as Wanda admired the spring roses along Hazel's front sidewalk. "I can't believe you are going to be sixty-four next month. Why, if I met you on the street, I'd guess you were in your early fifties, if that."

Wanda put her hand to her cheek to stop the blush, just as she had done then. But dressed in her lavender linen suit with the floral shell in shades of plum and raspberry, she had to admit she looked great. Especially since she had lost thirty pounds thanks to her best friend, Betty Sue Simpson's coaching and Zelda's Zumba classes twice a week. Exercise and a low carb, high protein diet worked. And for once, she'd stuck it out for more than two weeks.

"Bye Sophie." Wanda patted the dachshund on her velvety head and closed the backdoor, locking it. Two years ago, she never would have thought such measures necessary, but she had to face it. Scrub Oak had lost its tiny, secure community image. With growth came crime but also economic opportunities. Already three new establishments had opened downtown, two in recent weeks.

She allowed herself ample time to leisurely stroll the mile and a half trek to the newspaper office. Power walking in heels wouldn't do. No sense risking a sprained ankle or perspiration rings on her linen suit. She hoisted her handbag further into the crook of her elbow and breathed in the fresh spring air that flittered through the newly leafed treetops. Two squirrels zipped around a trunk of an elm tree as if they held the ribbons to a May Pole. A mockingbird sang its repertoire to fluff the feathers of some unknown female. The violet, buttery, and snow white irises along the walkway to Holy Hill Church, where she'd attended since third grade, were in full bloom. Gorgeous spring day.

Wanda glanced at the green, budding leaves on the trees in her neighborhood where once bare limbs hung. She clucked her teeth. *Change is the only certainty in this life so why do we resist it so much? Only God is eternal and unchanging.*

She trekked one more block to the newspaper's headquarters. Upon entering, she smiled at Tom's daughter, Vicki, who served as proofreader and receptionist.

"Hi, Mrs. Warn . . . um, Wanda." Vicki's face went from pale to red. "I keep doing that—calling you Mrs. Warner even though you told me to call you Wanda."

"Not to worry." She shrugged. "You were taught to respect your elders. Not many are these days."

"Well, perhaps I can remember not to be so formal after you meet with Daddy. At least I hope so."

What did she mean by that? Another flutter in Wanda's gut bumped against her yogurt and blueberries breakfast.

Vicki eased her body up from the secretary chair, arching her back to offset her bulging belly.

"My, that little one inside is definitely growing. Need help?"

"No, I'm fine. Six more weeks." She let out an elongated sigh and rubbed the bump. "Seems an eternity."

"Yes, I recall. The last trimester does seem to drag."

"I almost wish little Ian would come tomorrow. It's not yet ninety degrees out there and I already feel like an oven. Come June 18th, I may be roasting."

Wanda laughed. "Well, you do have a bun in the oven, as they say." She bent slightly to pat Vicki's tummy. "To think you and Mason have been married eighteen months. I recall your wedding as if it were *last* month."

"I do, too." Tom stood in the doorway to his office and held out his hand. "Best day of my life seeing my daughter marry, next to my own traipse down the aisle of course."

Shaking his hand with a firm grip, Wanda grinned. "How is Misty?"

"Fine. She will be even better if you agree to my offer. Please, come in." He motioned for her to enter his domain.

Vicki's grin widened as she joined them.

Wanda slowed her step. Okay, these hints did pique her curiosity yet also raised her concern. Especially when she noticed Mason, Vicki's husband and the newspaper's co-editor, already seated opposite Tom's desk.

What did these three have in mind and why did it concern her, a sixty-something widow?

Julie B Cosgrove

CHAPTER 2

Mason stood as she crossed the threshold.

"Here, Wanda. Have a seat." He held the chair for her.

"Appreciate it. What's this all about?" She swiped her palms down her skirt as she slid into the wooden seat and crossed her legs at the ankles, tucking them slightly to the side. Something her mother had drummed into her head since the age of seven, though back then her feet didn't touch the ground, so she curled one toe around the chair leg. Since she felt as if she'd been sent to the principal's office, she almost did so again today.

Tom returned to his executive chair. "I don't believe in beating bushes. So, let's get straight to the point."

"Thank you." *Or the jumbled breakfast in my stomach might start it growling.* She gave him a soft smile.

"You know, Wanda, since my attack almost two years ago, Mason and Vicki have been basically running the weekly newspaper. And now, the new digital addition on Tuesdays is taking off. More and more, people want news quicker than once a week on Fridays."

"That they do." Mason offered his pregnant wife his seat and then went to lean against a file cabinet. "Which is why we are changing the name to simply *The Oakmont Gazette*. Dropping the weekly part."

Wanda tucked her lips together and bobbed her head ever so slightly. What did this possibly have to do with her?

"Well, Misty has been nagging at me to retire and as an anniversary surprise, that is what I plan to do. First, on Monday I am taking her to New York for a weeklong shopping spree. Pray for me." He stood then pulled out the inner lining of his slack pockets to show them empty.

Everyone chuckled at his gesture to claim he had no money. Of course, he did. He had two successful businesses in town—the newspaper and the thrift shop.

Tom sat down again and continued. "Then the next week, we're heading on a three-week cruise through the Caribbean islands with our best friends, the Rollins. We'll be back in plenty of time for little Ian's arrival, though. Wouldn't miss my first grandchild's entry into the world." He flashed his daughter a wink.

"That's wonderful." A smile eased across Wanda's cheeks as she glanced at Vicki and Mason, but her mind whirled with even more questions.

Tom sat back and laughed. "I can see your wheels spinning. What does this have to do with you, and why did I ask you to come in today, right?'

She recrossed her legs. "For starters, yes."

He cleared his throat. "*The Gazette* will continue to produce the Friday editions in paper copies. Our seasoned citizens prefer print. They want to hold the paper, clip coupons, that sort of thing. We get that." Tom glanced at Mason. "But we want both editions to be online now as well."

"However," Mason interrupted. "We want to appeal to all ages and interests. Vicki and I adamantly want the newspaper to be a family affair. Family, as you can guess, is of *growing* importance to us."

Vicki patted her baby bump and they all laughed at Mason's pun.

Tom's chair screeched as he leaned forward and rested his hands on his desk. "We have obtained rights to a weekly crossword puzzle and Mason has designed it to be digitally workable. People will be able to type in their answers and even delete them if they make an error."

"Wow." Wanda felt her eyelids widen as her mouth formed an 'o'. "Good for you, Mason. You are becoming quite the geek."

He laughed. "Here is where, we hope, you fit in. Todd told us over dinner a few weeks ago how you and he solve the word games in the Fort Worth paper and have done so as long as he can recall. And, that you are quite the wiz."

Darn if her cheeks didn't warm at the compliment. She took a deep breath. "I have always loved words. We are blessed to know English because it has so many words rooted in other languages. It makes wordplay games much more fun."

Mason's captivating grin widened. "Exactly. We believe families should interact more. But kids are so digitally oriented these days, it tends to socially isolate them despite their ties to social media."

Wanda sighed. How many times had she seen families in local restaurants, each bent over tiny glowing screens rather than engaging in conversation? It never occurred to her they'd do the same at home. How sad.

"We hope by offering word games in the paper this can help them bond again, just as it has with you and your nephew. And he's turned out pretty well."

"Yes, he has." An almost parental pride rose in her heart. Mason and Todd had gone through school together and she knew Mason recalled how moody and troubled Todd had been as a teen when his parents went through the nastiest divorce in Scrub Oak history. Todd had ended up in her home and under her wing.

"The crossword puzzle will be good, but we'd like to offer even more." Mason shifted his eyes to his father-in-law and then back to Wanda. "We'd like to hire you parttime to design some word puzzles. Word searches, maybe even Hangman. How many words can you make from another word, that sort of thing." He motioned with his hand as if trying to glean the title from the atmosphere.

"Words-in-Word." Wanda nodded.

Tom pointed at her. "Yes, and that's exactly what we can call it. Agreed, Mason and Vicki?"

They both nodded.

His grin widened even more. "Mason is confident he can program these to be interactive so families can either play them online or solve them by pencil from the printed newspaper."

Wanda swallowed the lump that jolted in her throat. She opened her mouth but no words squeezed out.

Mason chuckled. "Wanda do you need a glass of water? I have rarely seen you at a loss for words."

He opened the mini fridge tucked in the credenza and pulled out a bottle for her and one for his pregnant wife, unscrewing the tops to both as a courtesy.

Tom continued. "We would like you to create these for both the Tuesday and the Friday editions. Could you manage that?"

Wanda sipped the cold, refreshing liquid. As it cascaded past her tonsils, her voice gained strength. "I'd . . . I'd be honored."

A secret dream of hers came to fruition with her response. No one, except perhaps God, ever knew of her desire to create word games. Wow. She took another gulp to keep her enthusiasm from bubbling over into a squeal of delight.

Tom clapped his hands together. "Excellent. Since I am on the way out, I will leave it to you three to work out the details." He rose from his desk and grabbed his sports jacket. "And now if you'll excuse me, I am taking my wife to brunch at the Woodway Grill and present her with our anniversary itinerary."

Wanda set the plastic bottle down, rubbed her fingers across her skirt one more time, and shook his hand with a grin so large her cheeks hurt. If she had not been tethered to his grip, she may have floated right through the ceiling like a sixty-something Mary Poppins.

Then a prickly thought popped her ballooning excitement. Lately, word games had led to crime clues. *Please, Lord, not again.*

CHAPTER 3

While at *The Gazette*, Wanda signed the contract to submit two different word games for each edition. Words-in-Word would be easy enough. But Hangman had to be designed a bit differently. Each edition would provide another clue, and the answer would contain a letter in the Hangman master word. The readers would have two guesses each time. A wrong answer would mean they had to add another body part to the stick man.

Digitally it would not be an issue. The program would automatically add the next body parts—head, torso, legs, and then arms, for a total of six clues. But for the paper editions, the honor system would have to be applied. Wanda hoped most of the people in their area would comply and not cheat. Of course, they would. They lived in Scrub Oak after all.

She borrowed an open desk next to the supply shelves

in the corner, which they stated would be hers from now on, and decided on *tablecloth* as the Words-in-Word puzzle for Friday. The word had been on the forefront of her mind because she had volunteered to wash and iron eight for the church women's spring luncheon.

Then she whipped up a Hangman puzzle that would be solvable in six clues over the next three weeks. The Friday paper edition would contain two clues to keep up with the digital subscriptions emailed out on Tuesdays and Fridays.

Both Mason and Vicki approved. The first clue would run in this Friday's paper, both the street copy and online edition along with instructions and an explanation. By next Monday morning, she'd create two more clues to the Hangman puzzle and submit two Words-in-Word ones.

Vicki's face lit up. "What if we had a contest of who could make the most words? People could email in or drop off their entries."

"Brilliant." Mason gave her a thumbs up. "That might drum up interest."

Wanda snapped her fingers. "We could have two winners per week. Then once a month we could have a drawing from those eight winners. I could talk with some of the local merchants about donating a gift card as a prize."

Mason patted her on the back. "Excellent. With you two ladies' ideas, subscriptions are going to soar."

Wanda's feet barely touched the concrete as she walked to Sally's Salads to meet Betty Sue for lunch. Before they lined up for the salad buffet, Wanda spurted out her news.

"Amazing. How wonderful. Right up your alley." Her friend's eyes widened in delight.

That's what Wanda loved about Betty Sue. Encouraging others seemed to be her main motive in life. Probably the reason she remained one of the most popular teachers in Scrub Oak despite the fact she'd retired five years ago.

Wanda took a tray and placed her chilled salad plate on it along with some silverware. "I already designed the first Hangman game and gave them a list of words to be used in the Words-in-Word. The initial clues will be in the paper this Friday."

Betty Sue's mouth opened so wide, Wanda almost felt like tossing cucumber slices in it, sort of like a cornhole game. But she resisted.

Sally, overhearing their conversation as she added more shredded carrots to the buffet entrees, let off a squeal. "Hey, everyone. Guess what? Wanda Warner is the new word puzzle creator for *The Gazette*."

Applause echoed through the small bistro.

Wanda felt her cheeks sizzle with pride. Her face spanned the room mouthing a "thank you" then she ducked her head and spooned some pumpkin seeds on top of her spring mix.

Choosing one of the chairs at a table for two, Betty Sue sat and placed her paper napkin in her lap. "So, how does it feel to be on staff at the newspaper?"

How indeed? "Surreal. Like a dream come true. And yet, I'm a bit nervous." Wanda set down her tray and took the other chair.

"Why?" Betty Sue forked a piece of curly kale and pushed the leaf in her mouth.

"Because word games seem to lead to clues for crimes lately. At least for me."

"Nonsense." Betty Sue shook her head. One eyebrow peaked in the teacher expression that probably made many of her students pay attention over the decades. "Word solving has given you a sharp and detail-seeking mind, which also lends itself to crime solving."

"We'll see," Wanda hissed under her breath as she took a bite of a keto-friendly, blueberry-lemon muffin, which tasted surprisingly wonderful.

Her friend tapped the rim of Wanda's plate with her butter knife. "Eat your salad. Not another word."

Wanda opened her mouth to laugh at the pun, but taking in the seriousness on Betty Sue's face, she chose discretion instead.

Keto Friendly
Lemon Blueberry Muffins

Ingredients:

- 2 c. Blanched Almond flour (You can use coconut flour, but I prefer almond. Or try CarbQuik—a Bisquick substitute—don't use the baking powder, though.)
- 1 c. of Organic Valley Whipping Cream
- ¼ c. unsalted butter
- 2 large eggs, whisked until creamy yellow
- 1 c. of Swerve granulated erythritol
- 1 Tbsp baking powder
- ½ c. fresh blueberries
- ½ Tbsp lemon zest
- ½ Tbsp lemon juice or extract
- ¼ tsp of salt – I use the potassium enriched low salt.

Directions:

1. Preheat oven to 350° F.
2. Melt butter in the microwave and slightly cool for 10 minutes, then add whisked eggs, stirring constantly for consistency.
3. Add the remaining ingredients and fold until well combined.
4. Pour into 12 silicone baking cups or a butter-lined 12-cup baking tin. You can use the paper muffin cups, but they may stick a bit when peeled away.
5. Bake for 25-30 minutes until golden brown and a

toothpick stuck into the center comes out clean.

6. Serve warm.

You can use cupcake muffin top pan (five-inch round) to make these as well. They turn out like thick blueberry pancakes, great with a lather of softened cream cheese!

CHAPTER 4

In fact, not to jinx anything, though she truly trusted in God's providence, Wanda decided not to mention her new task to Todd, who always stopped by to play Scrabble with her on Thursday mornings before going on second shift duty as a Scrub Oak patrolman. Not that she enjoyed keeping things from him. But he, above anyone else, knew how her love for words had led to crime-solving clues in the past.

He kept eying her over the kitchen table but she kept tight lipped.

"Something bothering you?"

"No. All is well. I do have news but I can't tell you about it yet. Perhaps in a day or two. Nothing bad." She hoped.

He shifted in his chair. "Okay."

Her mind would not stay on the game and he beat her

by 76 points. He rose, kissed her cheek, and whispered in her ear. "I hope you can concentrate better next week after the first clues appear in the paper tomorrow."

What? She twisted toward him, mouth pried to respond.

"Everyone will enjoy them, Aunt Wanda. No worries."

With a wink, he left out her backdoor.

Her mouth finally closed. Of course, he knew. By now the whole town did. They lived in Scrub Oak after all.

Wanda logged onto her computer and pulled up *The Gazette's* Friday digital edition. Her eyes danced over the computer screen. Mason did an amazing job with the graphics. She especially liked the turn-the-page feature, similar to the ones in e-book programs.

An article caught her eye. The Scrub Oak High School's spring concert was coming up on Saturday evening at seven. She'd need to get a ticket to that. Maybe Betty Sue would like to join her. On the next virtual page, the honor students for the fifth six weeks were listed, as were the basketball and baseball scores from the area schools. Looked like the high school team might be headed for the state playoffs. *Good.*

"Well, Sophie." Wanda patted the pooch who had laid

her chin on Wanda's foot. "Families love to see their kids' names in print. Vicki and Mason are truly doing a good job revitalizing the paper."

She swiped her mouse to turn to the next page. An interview with Pat Farmer, the new manager of the Ferguson Mansion, now a posh Bed and Breakfast, piqued her interest. After a long court battle, the heirs had finally sold the ten-bedroom monstrosity to an investor from Dallas. The murders that tainted its nouveau riche history lent to public curiosity. Already ghost tours through the wine cellars and hedge-maze had become quite a lucrative tourist attraction. Though some people in town, including Wanda's next door neighbor and close friend Evelyn, thought it a tad fiendish.

At last, on the back page sat the Word Puzzles. She tapped her foot in excitement, catapulting Sophie's chin by mistake. The dog grunted a low growl, and sauntered to her doggie bed

"Sorry, girl."

There they were. Her contributions. Wanda herself had come up with 17 words with three or more letters gleaned from the letters in *tablecloth* in the allotted 30 minutes. It would be interesting to see what words others submitted, and how many would enter the contest each day.

Then a smile spread across her cheeks as she noticed the Hangman puzzle. The graphics were superb. She bet

Vicki had a hand in the design. It pictured a wooden, L-shaped scaffold with the rope tied into a noose. Sprigs of grass sprouted from the base, along with a few bluebonnets, the state flower of Texas. Brilliant! No sense in making it gory.

The main clue was: *Where buns and babies-to-be are found.* There were six blank spaces. Over the next six clues, people would discover the answer to be *an oven.* One letter would be revealed in each day's puzzle.

The first letter's clue read: *One of the letters in the word that describes the road between streets where everyone places their trash cans.* Of course, the answer would be *alley,* which would correspond to the "a" in the main answer. Sure, it would be easy to solve, but they wanted to gain interest, not frustrate people. She ran her finger over the screen and prayed people would like these puzzles. Not for her glory, of course, but to help reconnect families. That led to reconnecting communities. And Scrub Oak's community lay dearly in her heart. Always had.

Perhaps being the puzzle creator for *The Gazette,* her secret dream, would in a backwash way get her even more positive notice. The applause in Sally's had made her optimistic. Was it prideful to hope for that? If so, she asked God to forgive her.

Over the years she had gotten a bad reputation for being a busy body. Just recently people's views had begun to change as she formed the neighborhood watch teams and became instrumental in catching a few bad guys around town. It hadn't hurt her nephew's standing in the community either now that he'd returned as one of the town's finest. He hadn't exactly been the hometown hero when he left for college.

Then her cell phone chime interrupted her thoughts. She recognized the ringtone for Betty Sue. "Good morning. What's up?"

"Did you hear? Anne Graves, owner of the new restaurant, Good Gravy, was robbed."

"Inside the restaurant?" How had they gotten in? Had they hidden in it all night?

"No. While walking to her car with the contents of the till from the previous night. Somebody smacked her from behind with a trash can lid, snatched the bank bag, and dashed down the alley."

The *alley*?

Wanda groaned.

Julie B Cosgrove

CHAPTER 5

Wanda sloughed off the creepy tingles that inched up her arms. Coincidence. Had to be.

"When did this happen?"

"Just now." Betty Sue's voice revved up a notch. "We heard her scream as we came out of Zumba. Luckily, the blow only stunned her. Doc Morgan is checking her out, though."

Wanda rubbed her forehead. "Did you see the first Hangman puzzle in the paper?"

"Wanda. This is not the time to gloat. A citizen in our town has been assaulted." Betty Sue's voice took on her stern educator tone.

She sighed through her nose. "I'm not gloating." Hadn't she just prayed about that? "It's only that . . . well, the answer happens to be *alley*."

"Oh." Her best friend's voice became silent. Then she

whispered. "I see."

Another groan gurgled up into Wanda's throat. "It's happening again, isn't it?"

"Surely not. I mean nobody would connect the two, would they?"

"I don't know. Both occurred today." She rose, tucked the cell phone between her shoulder and her left ear, and grabbed the bottle of ibuprofen from the cupboard. "I better call Mason and Vicki, just in case."

"Okay. But, Wanda?"

"Yeah?'

"Seriously. No one in their right mind would associate the two."

"Let's pray not. Bye." She poured herself a glass of water and swallowed down the medicine, hoping it would quickly ease the growing pressure in her temples.

Sophie raised her head, whimpered, then settled back in her doggie bed with one paw over her eyes.

"Thanks for the vote of confidence." Wanda shook her head and walked to her bedroom to get dressed. She chose a pair of tan slacks and a navy blouse then slipped into them.

She hopped on one foot, putting on her shoe as she spoke into the speaker app on her phone. "Vicki. I just heard about Anne Graves."

"Yes, thanks. Mason is already at the scene." Her voice sounded energetic, not hesitant or filled with doom and gloom. Did she not connect the dots yet?

Wanda gave up trying to get the shoe on while standing. She didn't need a tumble and broken hip. She sat on the edge of the bed, then pulled the strap over her heel. "Vicki, think of where it occurred. An alley."

"Oh, you mean like where Evelyn was whacked when *The Gazette* was trashed and where you were once kidnapped? I see how that could be upsetting."

Had to be pregnancy brain affecting Vicki. Wanda flopped back on the mattress and tried to control her tone. "True enough. Alleys seem to be the prime choice of thieves in this town. But Vicki, what also does it remind you of, especially . . . today of all days?"

Silence, then a soft, "Oh."

"Exactly. The first clue in the Hangman puzzle."

"Wanda I seriously doubt anyone will make the connection. I mean it's a common word." Her voice lilted, almost into a giggle.

Not the emotion Wanda expected from her. Perhaps her hormones were out of whack.

A phone rang in the background. Wanda recognized it as *The Gazette's* landline. Vicki's tone became hurried. "Hey, I gotta go. Talk later. Don't worry."

"Easier said . . ." Wanda sighed as she ended the call and glanced at the alarm clock on her bedstand. It read 10:55 AM. Even though his shift ended at five this morning, Todd might be awake. She speed dialed his cell phone number.

"Hey, Aunt Wanda." His voice sounded gravelly.

"Sorry. I woke you, didn't I?"

He grunted. "It's okay. I'm meeting Rebecca for lunch in an hour, so my alarm was set to go off in four minutes anyway."

Aw, progress. Rebecca had been an unreachable cheerleader in high school that he'd secretly crushed on. Lately the situation seemed reversed, since she and Vicki had become closer friends, which meant she frequented Scrub Oak more. "Oh, where?"

"That new place. Good Gravy."

"Well, about that . . ." She quickly explained about the robbery.

"Wow. I guess it's all under control or Chief Brooks would have called me in. They will still be open, right?"

He didn't get it either. Maybe she was being slightly paranoid. Then again, he had just woken up and probably hadn't seen the first Hangman clue in the paper. So, she told him about it.

"Aunt Wanda, congrats. Truly."

"Yes, but the first clue matches what happened." She clutched her fists.

"Kinda a stretch don't you think?"

"I would, if in the past two years Scrabble words hadn't led to clues in a series of murders, or those notes on cars led to a kidnapping, or the palindrome graffiti that led to . . ."

"Okay, okay. I get it." Frustration rang in his voice. "Stop worrying. I am confident this is pure speculation."

"You honestly think so?"

"Aunt Wanda, bask in your new accomplishment. People are going to love these newspaper word games. Don't try to sabotage it with negative thoughts."

When did her nephew get so wise? "I suppose you're right."

His breathing calmed a bit. "Look, I need to call Good Gravy anyway to make sure they will be open for lunch and then talk with Rebecca. Even if they are, she may want to eat someplace else. I'll see what I can find out."

A bit of relief loosened the tight grip her emotions had on her tummy. "Thanks, Todd. I really appreciate it."

He chuckled. "Love ya. Now, go grab a nice lunch with Evelyn at the Hook & Owl and enjoy the rest of your day."

She giggled. "Oh, I see. Stay away from Good Gravy you mean. I wouldn't think of spying on you, dear nephew."

He paused. "Of course not. You're never inquisitive, are you?"

His playful sarcasm dripped through the receiver.

She laughed and said goodbye, then called Evelyn. He and Betty Sue were correct. What happened in the past didn't dictate the here and now. If Anne had parked down the street from her restaurant instead of the alley no alarms would have gone off in Wanda's head.

Coincidence. Pure and simple.

She grabbed her purse and left after making sure Sophie had enough water in her bowl and a rawhide treat to gnaw on. Right on time, Evelyn pulled out of her garage next door. Wanda got into the passenger side.

They got to the pub and sat by the window looking out onto the square. Behind the bar that only served coffee, lemonade, and tea until five o'clock in the afternoon, the TV blared the local news from the DFW Metroplex. The female reporter's voice hit Wanda's ear. "Elsewhere in the Metroplex, restaurant owner Anne Graves was assaulted and robbed in an alleyway behind her restaurant in the small town of Scrub Oak near Cleburne. This is the third violent incident in an alley of the small community in two years."

The camera cut away to Anne seated on the curb with a gel pack to the back of her head and an EMT attendant taking her blood pressure. She spoke into a microphone with the TV station's name on it. "Guess small towns are not as quiet as they used to be. I moved here to get away from crime. Who knew I'd be a victim of one?"

Evelyn gaped. "Good heavens. Are you calling a special meeting of the neighborhood watch captains?"

Wanda felt the blood leave her face. She had been so caught up in herself she totally neglected to consider her town or the responsibility she had to its citizens as organizer of the watch teams.

"I suppose I should." She instantly sent texts to the four captains asking them to meet at her house at seven-thirty that evening. Glancing up from her phone's screen she motioned with her head at her neighbor. "You are welcome to come."

"I'm not a captain yet. Though when Collin Rollins resigns soon, I might think about it."

Wanda nodded as she sipped her iced tea. "I hope you will. By the way, he and Claudia are going on a cruise through the Caribbean islands with Tom and Misty Jacobs. They both got married twenty-five years ago, two weeks apart. Misty and Tom arrived back from their honeymoon just in time for Claudia and Collin's rehearsal dinner. They were their best man and matron of honor. Seems like yesterday."

"So, I heard." Evelyn leaned in. "Guess who is minding the Cut Above while Claudia is gone?"

"Who?" Wanda waited as her friend licked her lips. Her eyes glowed, Wanda suspected because for once Evelyn knew something before she did.

"Rebecca Epson."

Wanda's jaw swung open. "She's going to cut hair?"

"Of course not. She's a schoolteacher in Cleburne for goodness' sake. But it lets out in two weeks. No, she will just answer the phones, make appointments, that sort of thing. Claudia's two assistants, Isabel and Brittanie, will be filling in. Still, Rebecca will be staying at the Collin's home to babysit their cats."

Aw, which meant she'd probably see a lot more of Todd. That could get interesting. Wanda masked the grin growing on her lips by dabbing her mouth with her napkin.

Evelyn caught it, though, and winked.

CHAPTER 6

Wanda remained quiet during the rest of the meal. She heard Evelyn's conversations enough to give short replies but her mind filled with all sorts of what-if scenarios. One thing for certain, she had to meet Anne Graves and ask her about the incident.

The stylish lady had recently moved to Scrub Oak from San Antonio to be nearer to her daughter and grandkids in Dallas. That's what Priscilla at the Coffee Bean told her. They both lived in the condos a block from Wanda. Wanda had seen Anne around town the past few weeks and often nodded a friendly howdy to her. But they had never really chatted.

What could she take her as an introductory gift? Not a casserole or dessert. As restaurant owner, Anne might not appreciate that, particularly if it happened to taste better than one of her recipes. Maybe a nice potted plant for her establishment? That might work.

"Ev, would you mind dropping me off at Kay's? I want to pick up some flowers, or maybe a house plant."

"What's the occasion?"

"Just a *Welcome to Scrub Oak* gift."

Evelyn almost dropped her car keys as they walked to her subcompact. "For Rebecca?"

Wanda waved that thought away with her hand as if erasing the assumption. "No, no. Someone else. I have decided as neighborhood watch chairperson, I should greet our newcomers and let them know the name and phone number of their captain. In fact, I plan to bring that up at the meeting tonight."

"Uh, huh." Evelyn clicked the key fob to unlock her car doors.

Wanda halted before opening the passenger side. "What's that supposed to mean?"

Evelyn waggled her finger at her. "I know you, Wanda Lee Warner. You are headed to Anne Graves' restaurant, aren't you?"

Caught in the act. Wanda pressed her lips together and shrugged.

"Well, then I'm going with you. It'll be less suspicious. I guess I will be her watch captain now that Collin is resigning, so . . ."

"Ah, so you agree to take it on. Great." Wanda winked and slid inside her friend's car.

They picked out a spathiphylum, otherwise known as a closet lily. The dark shiny leaves and exotic white blooms flourished in indoor lighting. Kay wrapped the cream-colored pot in a chestnut foil and added a sandy colored bow. "It's the colors in her restaurant. Off-white, tan, and a rich brown. The colors of various gravies."

"Oh. What a cute idea. Gravies for country fried steaks, chicken, and beef. How yummy." Evelyn licked her lips as she pointed to each hue. The fact she'd just downed a bowl of stew and two helpings of soda bread didn't matter. The woman was always ready to eat, and she never gained an ounce.

Wanda shook her head. "So, you've eaten there, Kay?"

Kay tilted her head as she fluffed the bow. "Oh, yes. The food is quite good. Especially the glazed carrots." She slapped on a gold sticker with her flower shop's name on it, rang up the purchase, and handed the plant to Wanda. "Tell her 'hi' for me."

Good Gravy sat in the next block where Carl's Used Cars had once been. The enterprising lady had renovated the showroom and offices into her establishment and allowed the car lot to be used for parking, not only for her clientele but those going to the Bargain Boutique or Harry's Hardware Haven. Doing so reduced the congestion from street parking around the square. Community minded and smart. Wanda admired her for that.

Evelyn held the door as Wanda entered with the plant. The cozy but chic atmosphere immediately welcomed her. Quiet piano music set the mood. The walls were decorated in an off-white pattern-on-pattern wallpaper and the floors in a creamy marble with small veins of golden brown and sienna.

Simple brass chandeliers hung about the room. Wait staff were dressed in dark sienna. Bronzed Texas stars and cattle scenes decorated the walls. A few late-lunch patrons sat at tables with ivory tablecloths draped over chestnut or sand-colored ones with matching cloth napkins.

An icy sensation raced up Wanda's spine like a subzero zipper against her skin. The Words-in-Word puzzle had been *tablecloth*. No, that had to be a stretch of the imagination to assume there'd be a connection.

"May I help you?" A woman of graceful stature with bobbed, collar-length white hair greeted them with a dazzling smile.

Wanda shifted the plant to her left arm and extended her right hand. "Are you Anne?"

"Yes, I am. And you are?"

"Wanda Lee Warner and this is Evelyn Jacobs. We apologize for the delay in welcoming you to Scrub Oak. I am chairperson of the neighborhood watch program and Evelyn will soon be captain for your area."

"I see. I wished I'd met you before this morning." She

raised a delicate hand to the back of her head.

"So, we heard. We can't be everywhere but now you know who to call if anything occurs again. Which of course, is unlikely . . ." She swallowed back the awkwardness and handed the restaurant owner a card with her name and number on it.

"Oh, well, let's hope not, right?" Anne tucked the card in her pocket and eyed the plant with a half-smile. "Did you bring this lovely greenery for me?"

Evelyn snatched the potted plant from Wanda's grip and handed it to the proprietor. "Yes. Kay decorated it in your colors. We hoped it might brighten your day and that you might find a place for it." She glanced around the room.

"Absolutely. How kind of you." Anne set it on the register counter and stood back with her hands clasped. "There. It's perfect, don't you think?"

Wanda agreed. "I am so relieved to see you are all right. We heard on the midday news about your harrowing experience."

"Yes, but the incident is over and there is no sense belaboring the point, is there? May I offer you ladies coffee, perhaps a dessert? On the house." Anne motioned to a table for two at the back.

"Sure. Whatcha got?" Evelyn grinned.

Wanda decided on decaf and Evelyn ordered a slice of pecan pie topped with a scoop of vanilla bean ice cream.

Anne brought it on a square, cream-colored plate with drizzles of dark chocolate over it. She handed them each a mug of coffee then set one down for herself. "You offer me a chance to get off my feet. I think I am still a bit shaken."

"Please join us. And tell us what happened." Wanda put on her best sympathetic expression. Something about the warmth and grace of this new lady in town clutched her heart. "Unless you are tired of repeating it."

"No, it's okay. Though several of my customers have inquired about it as well as the police, the reporters . . ." She rubbed her scalp and winced. "I still have a pretty large goose egg on the back of my head. That guy came out of nowhere. He must have been crouched down behind the garbage cans."

"Wasn't wearing a black hoodie by any chance?" Evelyn grimaced. Almost two years ago, her assailant in an alley had been dressed that way.

"No, one of those ski masks. You know knitted with holes for the eye and mouth." She ran her thumb over her mug. "Red, with white deer in a pattern on it. Funny, I just recalled that."

Wanda patted her hand. "Sometimes it takes a while for the brain to assimilate all the information. Is there anything else you recall now that you didn't before?"

Anne took a sip and set the coffee down. "Let me see. He—I keep saying that. I really can't be sure. The person had to be taller than me, don't you think? But I guess most men would be. But then so could some women. I am only five-foot-four."

"Sure, I'm five-six." Evelyn smiled as she dug her fork into the pie. "But I promise you, it wasn't me."

"Of course not." Anne snickered. "Let's see. What else? I imagine he or she had to be athletic. The blow knocked me to my knees. Plus, this person dashed away quickly. Rounded the corner before I could scream out, 'Hey, come back here.' At least I think that's what I called out."

"What else did he or she wear?" Wanda peered over her steaming mug.

"Hmmm. Dark jeans. A T-shirt. V-necked, I think. Tennis shoes." Her eyes widened. "Oh. Bright turquoise on the soles. I recall that now."

"Very good." Wanda grinned.

"I should call the police and let them know what I've remembered, right?"

"No need. I've just recorded it in my notebook. Hi, Aunt Wanda."

The three women jolted to see Todd standing there in uniform. He tapped the rim of his Stetson in greeting but then narrowed his gaze directly at his aunt.

Wanda almost slid under the table.

Julie B Cosgrove

CHAPTER 7

That night at the captain's meeting, all agreed to spread the word to the volunteer watch people in their sectors—be on the lookout for anyone wearing tennis shoes with turquoise soles. Then they approved the sending of a welcome basket or gift to newcomers, either residents or businesses.

Collin Rollins raised his hand. "How do we pay for it, though?"

"Easy. We don't." Wanda smirked as murmurs of confusion floated around her living room. "Tomorrow I am visiting area merchants and requesting they offer a gift card or certificate to winners of the new word game puzzles in *The Gazette*. I'll ask them if they want to also contribute something for newcomers. It will be good advertising for them."

All four captains gave her a thumbs up.

W₄

Saturday morning Wanda visited The Bird's Nest, run by Gail Longoria who possessed a passion for environmental causes, especially birds. The shop sold everything from feeders to seeds to contracted artwork depicting birds. Part of her profits went to wildlife preservation. She'd opened a couple of months ago on the first day of spring, but Wanda had never officially introduced herself.

Wanda brought her a Holy Hill cookbook, which the church ladies put together several years ago to help fund a new roof. She also brought her a bouquet of six salmon-colored roses, courtesy of Hazel Perk's front yard. With Hazel's permission, of course.

"Hi, I'm Gail. Welcome to the Bird's Nest." The petite raven-haired lady with a beak-like nose and wearing a peacock colored blouse greeted her and graciously accepted the gifts.

"I apologize for not dropping by sooner."

"Not at all." She placed the roses on the counter. "How kind of you. I have wanted to become more involved in the community but the first few months of a new business suck up so much time."

"Well . . ." Wanda glanced around the shop once again. "I may have an idea." She hadn't planned on hitting up the proprietor just yet for a donation, but when God cracks open a door . . .

Thrilled at the suggestion, Gloria offered to provide a plastic bird feeder, filled with seed, to each new resident and a bird calendar for each business. Winners of the word puzzles would receive a gift certificate.

Wanda thanked her for the generous gift offers and bought a book on the migratory birds of Texas. Then she visited the Hoot and Owl one block over. Ray O 'Malley offered a coupon for a free dessert and drink with the purchase of a lunch or dinner to the newcomers and a free Sunday brunch to the word puzzle winner.

Beverly Newby of Anna's Antiques offered a discount on any purchase over twenty-five dollars along with a yearly subscription to Antiques Monthly online magazine to the town's newcomers and the same to a future word puzzle winner. She'd design the coupons on the computer and have them ready for Wanda in a few days.

More providence. Wanda caught Pat Farmer, the new manager of the Ferguson Mansion turned B&B, on the corner waiting for the walk sign to change. After a short chat, the proprietor decided to donate a free ghost tour of the wine cellar and maze to newcomers and a free night's stay to a future monthly prize winner. "They can use it for guests who come into town. It'll help spread the word." She clasped her hands in front of her and smiled.

Smart businesswoman. Plus, she had the demeanor of a genteel lady of the manor, perfect for running a B&B.

Wanda thanked her for her very charitable offer.

Mayor Arnold stopped Wanda on the curb on the way to Sally's Salads.

"I hear you are asking for donations for our newcomers and for the new word game puzzle winners. Great idea. The Chamber of Commerce will offer free Scrub Oak T-shirts and two hours free parking in the square to the town's newcomers, business or residential." He shook her hand, politician style—firm with a wink.

"I didn't know we had Scrub Oak T-shirts."

He chuckled. "We will soon enough. They will be for sale in time for May Fest at Sally's Salads, in the Coffee Bean at the Grocery Mart, Bargain Boutiques, and at Hardware Haven. Proceeds will go to funding new landscaping around the courthouse, the fountain, and the gazebo in the park. After last January's freak seven-day freeze, many of our shrubs died off."

May Fest lay just around the corner. Originally an annual Scrub Oak weekend event honoring the graduates of the local high school, it had become a week-long affair featuring several venues throughout the community. Downtown stores had sidewalk sales and the town square and parks offered activities in the evenings such as a concert, play, or fireworks.

Holy Hill, where Wanda attended, organized a kick-off hotdog cookout after Sunday services the weekend before graduation with a May Pole, cake walk, and cornhole games. The middle school always put on a play the Tuesday night before graduation. For the past few years, Evelyn's church offered Bingo, relay games, and a two-day garage sale on Wednesday and Thursday. The women's auxiliary's arts and crafts show on Friday always drew crowds to the town square. The elementary kids decorated the football field with homemade congratulation signs for the Saturday mid-morning pomp and circumstance.

She thanked the mayor for his generosity and added his items to her growing list of donations.

Within a few days, she'd gleaned quite a treasure trove from her fellow citizens, much more than she had anticipated. The townsfolk's generosity made Scrub Oak a special place to live all right. It put an extra bounce in her step as she dropped by *The Gazette* on Monday to share the news. Mason applauded her efforts and showed her his final touches to the Hangman clue scheduled for the Tuesday digital edition the next morning.

The clue for the word of the day read, "Where birds sleep." The four-letter answer of course was *nest*. In the interactive version, each wrong guess automatically moved a body part to the noose along with a caricature sound of "Uh-oh. Try again."

"Brilliant." Wanda clapped and danced on her toes. "Where is Vicki?"

"Checkup. We think the baby may be dropping." He fanned his face and gave her a smirk. "I'll be a daddy in a month or so I suspect. I hope not sooner. I haven't assembled the bassinette yet."

"Doc says best guess is three weeks so you better get hustling, honey." Vicki entered, set her purse down on the desk, then sniffled as her voice cracked. "If Ian comes when Mom and Dad are on their cruise, they will never forgive me."

Mason stood and came over to hug her. "They'll be back June fifth. That's three weeks from today. It'll all work out simply fine."

Vicki nodded with her head buried in his shoulder but continued to weep.

Sweet man. He knew her hormones rode a roller coaster right now. Wanda gave him a thumbs up and tiptoed out of the office.

CHAPTER 3

Tuesday morning, Wanda opened her laptop as she sipped her coffee and played the Hangman puzzle, purposely answering incorrectly to make sure the "uh-oh" sounded. It did, which made her jolt then giggle. *Perfect. Families will love this.*

She envisioned them sitting around the computer laughing and answering the way-too easy question. In a few weeks she'd make them a bit harder, but not too obscure. Satisfied, she closed her laptop and got on with her day.

After running a few errands, Wanda decided to eat at Good Gravy for lunch. Blackened chicken with the steamed broccoli and wild rice shouldn't add much to her slowly diminishing waistline.

Anne greeted her and offered her a table near the center of the restaurant.

"How's the headache?" Wanda slipped a napkin in her lap.

Anne snickered. "Better until I met with the bank. I'd hope to have my losses reimbursed by now but they have started their own investigation and that can take up to ten days."

"I'll be praying for you. It's tough just starting out."

Anne blushed and clutched the small filagree cross dangling just below her décolleté. "Thank you. I know God's got this, but it still gives me a touch of anxiety."

"Of course. You went through a horrid experience." Wanda touched the restaurant owner's sleeve. "Anything I can do, let me know."

Just then Fix-It Finn dashed inside. "Just heard on the police squawker. The Bird Nest has been robbed. They knocked poor Gloria out with a twenty-five-pound sack of sunflower seeds, snatched all the money in her till, and ran out the backdoor."

Gasps sounded all over the restaurant.

Wanda stared at her plate. No, no. Not possible. Coincidence that the answer to today's Hangman had been *nest,* right?

What if it wasn't? Would everyone suddenly blame her after all her effort to win favor in her community? Her heart crushed. The last bite of broccoli jumped back into her throat as she dashed to the restroom.

With all the composure she could muster, Wanda

returned to her table but asked them to package her meal to go then slithered out of the restaurant. Her cell phone chimed as she exited. Betty Sue's name came up.

"Did you hear the latest?"

How did her lifelong friend always get the news so quickly? "Yeah. And to think I just visited her shop a few days ago." Wanda sat on the bench outside the restaurant, the takeout bag dangling from her fingers.

She went on to explain to Betty Sue about the donations.

"That's great the merchants are being so generous. Good job." Her voice softened. "But Wanda, honey, the answer to today's Hangman was *nest*. And the Words-in-Word was *mockingbird*. You picked them, correct?"

"Sort of. I gave them all to Mason but he chose the order. Of course, he would go in the order I put them, though. And I guess subconsciously I matched each of the Words-in-Word to the Hangman clues." Wanda let out a guttural groan. "This can't be happening. It simply can't."

"Where are you? Do you want company?"

"No, that is sweet of you and I appreciate it but I need to find Todd." A sniffle caught in her throat. She swallowed it down and stood. "I'll call you later on, okay?"

"Promise? You know I'm here if you need me."

"Thanks, dear friend. You always have been."

She hung up and started to rise when Evelyn called.

"Yeah, I know." Wanda sighed and sat back down on the bench. "Weird, right?"

"More than weird. Almost clairvoyant. You haven't been playing with Ouija boards or anything have you? That's a sin, you know."

Evelyn tended to be very black and white about these things. At least she stuck to her beliefs. Wanda had to give her that.

"No, nothing so eerie. Listen, I've gotta go find Todd, Ev. I'll keep you posted."

She fought back the tears all the way to the police station.

Seeing her enter, Reagan cupped her hand over the black phone receiver. "Todd just came on duty. He's in his office."

Wanda nodded and padded down the hall, aware her rubber-soled shoes squeaked on the linoleum tiles. The rhythm of her footsteps squawked out a sound like "guilty, guilty." She halted, took a deep breath, and tapped on his door jamb.

Todd sat with his fingers tented. Jimmy Bob stood next to the desk.

"Hi, Aunt Wanda. Glad you came by. We need to talk."

She slumped into the chair feeling like a kid called to the principal's office. It had happened to her only once in her life, in fifth grade. Darryl Sanders had been whispering to Chuck Baker, who sat cattycorner behind her. Wanda, thinking Darryl had finally noticed she existed on this planet, kept trying to figure out what he cryptically said. It seems he passed the answers to the multiple choice test the teacher planned to give. The teacher caught her with one hand and yanked her by the ear while grasping Darryl in her other hand, impelling them down the hallway.

The principal punished them both with two weeks of detention and Chuck got away scot-free. Wanda hated Chuck the rest of the time they were in school for not stepping up and telling the truth. Every time they passed in the halls, she'd glare right into his soul. Thank goodness his family moved away.

But this was her nephew, whom she loved with all her heart, sitting opposite her. The one she had guided through his tumultuous teen years and encouraged through college and the police academy. The one who played Scrabble with her every Thursday in her kitchen over coffee.

Todd pulled up the word puzzles from Friday and split-screened them with today's entry. He swiveled the computer screen around for her to observe.

"I know." It came out in a squeak as if she'd swallowed a mouse.

"Wanna explain?"

"I can't, Todd. Honestly."

He glanced at Jimmy Bob who harumphed and left the room.

Todd scooted his chair back, came around the desk, and perched his hip on the edge. He took his aunt's hands. "You have to admit this is getting a tad bizarre."

"Agreed." She tried to swallow but her mouth had long since evaporated all the moisture on her tongue. She coughed into her elbow.

Todd released her hands and rose. "Be right back."

She fiddled with the strap of her purse and took deep breaths until he returned with a bottle of water. She took it and swigged several gulps. "Thanks. Same perp?"

He returned to his side of the desk. "Seems like it from Gloria's description. She didn't actually see who hit her from behind. She had her back turned, helping a customer decide which birdfeeder to buy and heard the shop door open. She called out she'd be only a minute, rang the customer's purchase, and then glanced around as the customer exited. No one else appeared to be in the aisles. She heard a noise near the shelves where the bulk seed is stocked, went to check, and wham."

"Did she catch a glimpse at least?"

"Only the turquoise soles of a pair of shoes dashing past her as she lay sprawled on the floor."

Wanda sighed.

Todd's chair creaked as he leaned back in it. "You don't have a pair that matches that description, do you?"

She gasped then saw his eyes twinkle. Ooh, that boy. He always knew how to get her goat.

"Like I could lift a twenty-five pound bag of seed." She let out a little chuckle then took another swig of the cold water. "I honestly don't know what to make of this, Todd. That's why I came here today. I need advice."

"I wish I had some. Thing is, Mrs. Longoria mentioned you had dropped by and had toured her shop recently."

"Is she accusing me of casing the joint? Todd, really." She crossed one leg over the other as she let of a small tsk, but inside her stomach reenacted an Olympic gymnast's floor routine.

"Not in so many words." He edged his chair further from the desk as if to put more distance between them.

Why?

Todd broke eye contact as he flipped his pen back and forth. "May I have the answers to the rest of the Hangman puzzle and the words you are considering for the next several Words-in-Word?"

Wanda tried to remain calm. He had a job to perform after all and couldn't show favorites. At least she assumed this had to be purely protocol. No way would he think otherwise.

"Sure, if Mason says it is okay. I need to ask him first."

"Okay. Call him."

She nodded. Then caught his eyebrow arch. "Oh, you mean now?"

"Yes ma'am. That is exactly what I mean."

She couldn't quite grasp the nature of his tone, but she knew she didn't like it. Not one bit.

CHAPTER 9

Mason answered on the fourth ring, a little out of breath. "Sorry. I was under the desk trying to reconnect the router. What's up?"

Seriously? Had he not heard? Wanda pushed her emotions back into her gut. These *coincidences* had shaken her sensibility. She put the call on speaker and set it down on Todd's desk. "Did you hear about the Bird's Nest?"

"Yeah, Vicki is over there now getting the scoop from Gloria Longoria, no pun intended."

Wanda chuckled knowing the merchant probably used a scoop to dole out the bird seed from the large commercial bins in her store. She waited for Todd to make the link. Obviously, he didn't. He remained stone-faced. "I am at the police station with Todd. He is concerned, and frankly so am I."

"About?"

She sucked in a deep breath. Did he really not have a clue? Maybe his daddy-to-be brain didn't run on all cylinders today. "That our word puzzle clues seem to precipitate crime, of course." Her tone had come out sharp, but she couldn't help it. "I'm sorry to jump down your throat, but this is disturbing."

She heard Mason pull out his executive chair and sit down. "I agree, but I have decided to play up the angle. That is one of the reasons Vicki is at the pet store now. It might create more interest in the paper."

Todd drew closer to the phone lying flat on his desk. "Exactly what do you mean, Mason?"

"Look, Todd. I am confident this is pure coincidence. An alley is a perfectly logical place for a crime to occur. If Ms. Graves had parked in the street, this would be a non-issue. And the fact that the word today was *nest* could have meant one in a tree, sitting in the park or the woods behind Ferguson's Mansion, under the rafters of the gazebo for goodness's sakes, or the one dangling out of the Grocery Mart's sign."

Wanda's hope perked. "I see what he is saying. It is like when people pick a Bible passage to support their point of view instead of having the passage guide their actions. We are looking at this after the fact and perhaps making a connection that isn't truly there at all."

Todd waggled his head back and forth. "Maybe. But I would still like access to the rest of the clues to this

Hangman puzzle and the ones my aunt has turned in for the Words-in-Word."

"For what purpose? To wait until the next crime occurs, if it does, and then try to find a word match?"

Todd sighed and sat back. "I see your point, Mason. Even so . . ."

"Todd, has there been any other crime reported between Tuesday and Friday?"

"Not out of the ordinary. The new high school principal's front yard was papered in the opposing team's colors after the baseball game. Sore losers. And the Edwards reported the neighbor's dog dug up their petunias again. Oh, and two kids were caught shoplifting popsicles from the Grocery Mart." He snickered. "They started to melt next to their skin under their T-shirts."

Wanda and Mason laughed as well.

"It's all in our biweekly report that Reagan will email you at *The Gazette*."

"Got it, Todd. What would we do without y'all?"

Wanda noticed Todd's cheeks darken, just a tad. "Keeps you from hacking into our computers my friend."

Mason laughed. "Look, I don't mind if you get the answers ahead of time, just don't try to draw conclusions that aren't there."

"Right. That's your job as reporters." Todd's tongue in cheek comment came through in his tone of voice.

"Anything to help drum up business for our town's

finest." Mason chuckled.

Wanda grinned at their banter. With young people like Todd, Mason, and Vicki now influencing their community, Scrub Oak would be just fine. She and her peers had raised the next generation well.

Todd snorted, then his tone took on a serious, police-like attitude. Probably the one he used to ask drivers for their license and insurance. "Mason, I get that this angle might sell subscriptions but I caution you to be careful. I don't want your article to influence public opinion too much. It might impede or falsely influence our investigation."

"You think the crimes are connected, don't you?"

"Early days, but yes. The descriptions both ladies gave, though vague, match. And the fact that both are women merchants and new ones in our community may be a factor. Talk later, Mason." He glanced at his aunt as he punched her phone to disconnect the call. "No offense about them being ladies."

"None taken. In fact, if I were Beverly or Sally, I'd be a bit nervous. I think I will talk to the neighborhood watch team in the downtown area about keeping an extra eye on their two establishments."

"Good idea, Aunt Wanda. Thank you." He reached in his desk and pulled out a notepad. "Do you recall the clues or do you need time to pull them up on your laptop?"

"I can access the file on my phone. I'm not totally

technically challenged." Wanda sighed and checked her tone. "Sorry. This has me upset."

His voice quieted. "I know."

She wrote out the rest of the clues and answers that made up the main answer to the Hangman and then tore off the piece of paper to hand to him.

Todd glanced at it. "This is really easy, Aunt Wanda."

"It is meant to be. We want to encourage families to get involved. They will get more challenging as time progresses."

"How did you come up with this?"

"I thought of Vicki sitting there rubbing her baby bump and talking about how she'd soon be roasting in the summer heat. We had laughed about her having a bun in the oven."

"I see, and the first letter in the answers all correspond to the letters in the final answer, then. An oven."

"Like I said, we wanted to make the first one easy."

"What if we mixed it up a bit? Not list the clues in order. Post the number six clue next."

Wanda thought about it. "I can't see that Mason will have an issue with that. Unless it affects his programing interactively. I don't know much about that part of the process. He's probably already formatted the next one for Hangman but I will check."

"What about the Words-in-Word clues?"

She wrote them down next. "They are not as easy as

to come up with, Todd. I must pick one that can break out into at least twenty other words consisting of three or more letters. The key is to include the most common letters."

"Ah, like on Wheel of Fortune. R, L N, S, T, and E."

Wanda winked as she tapped her temple. "I knew you graduated in the top five of your academy class for a reason."

Todd's face turned the color of Hazel's prize Chrysler Imperial roses.

"But not always. Mockingbird, for example." She reached and tapped the word with her forefinger. "Even so, there are over twenty-five words that can easily be gleaned from it and it is our state bird."

He nodded. "Thanks. Sorry to ask for these but . . ."

"No problem. I know you are just doing your job." *Now.* Wanda blew him a kiss and left the police station. Then she texted Mason. "Todd suggests we mix things up—list number six next for the Hangman game, then three, five, and four. Also mix up the Words-in-Word list I submitted a bit just in case."

A thumbs up emoji appeared on her screen. Then his response. *Have to go with the third Hang Man though. Already formatted. Then we'll do six, four, five. Will ask Vicki to pick the next Words-in-Word from the list you sent.*

CHAPTER 10

On Thursday morning, Todd appeared at her kitchen door with gluten-free blonde brownies. "I have no idea what these taste like, but they are supposed to be non-caloric and low carb according to Sally. They are made with almond flour and with monkey-something instead of sugar." He scrunched his nose.

Wanda laughed. "Monk fruit. Thanks. I've had them and they are good. You won't hardly taste the difference." She handed him a cup of coffee and waved for him to sit at the table. She'd already laid out the Scrabble game.

"We'll see." He shrugged and sat down to draw his wooden tiles. She always let him go first.

"Any progress on the investigation you can share?" She plated the brownies and put them on the table.

His eyes shifted briefly to her face and then back to the board. "As you know, there have been no further incidences. But then again, tomorrow is Friday isn't it? That's when the next Hangman clue appears."

She slapped his arm playfully. "Shush."

He snickered and took a bite of brownie. "Hmm, these aren't half bad."

"Told you." She chose her tiles and studied them.

"Seriously, thank the downtown neighborhood watch team for beefing up their presence. Who knows? It may have convinced whoever assaulted those two ladies that Scrub Oak is not the town to mess with."

"Amen!" Pride and loyalty swelled up like yeast dough in her heart "No clue as to who the assailant is, then?"

"At first we thought it might be an extraordinarily strong woman because of the color of the soles of the shoes. But our research online shows that several men's athletic shoes also come in similar colors. Also, in red, green, yellow, orange, purple . . ." He shrugged. "I had no idea."

Wanda snapped her fingers. "I recall that world-renown tennis player a while back who was banned from playing on some international court because of his orange shoes."

"Back in my day you had two choices, white and black." He sighed and played his first word.

"In your day?" Wanda laughed out loud. "You sound as if you are almost ready for the nursing home instead of me."

He peered into her face with love. "You? Not for another twenty years at least. You are still spry, witty, and youthful looking."

Wanda swiped the compliment away. "You sweet-talking boy. How was lunch with Rebecca? You never said."

"Fine." He dropped his focus to the tiles and began to rearrange them on the wooden stand. "She wanted my advice on whether or not to move into the Lakeview Apartments."

"Oh? I thought she was housesitting for the Rollins."

"She is, for now." He continued to study his letters. "But she's accepted a teaching position at Scrub Oak Elementary in the fall."

Wanda held her gasp in her throat. Stay cool. Don't speculate. But it sure sounded as if things between them had progressed in the right direction.

Todd huffed and lifted his eyes to hers. "Are you going to play or not?"

Oops. Message received. Not a subject he wished to pursue.

She placed a word off his that added thirty-two points to her score and smirked. "By the way, all the watch team members have been particularly aware of people's footwear, but no one has reported seeing sneakers like that."

"Yeah, neither have we. We asked Keith to be on the lookout at Better Burgers where so many folks hang out. I even spoke with Micky Lozano, the high school coach. He can't recall seeing any students wearing them, on or off the fields or courts."

"So, it isn't someone locally."

"That is my guess, Aunt Wanda. Which is good news, and then bad as well."

His comment confused her. She shook her head rapidly. "Why?"

"It widens our search parameters. The Metroplex is a large territory. Did you realize there are over 200 cities and towns in this area? The population is over seven and a half million people. That's almost as many as New York City."

"Good heavens. That many?" Wanda groaned. How could she possibly help Todd narrow his search? Only one way. Interview both Anne and Gloria again to see if either of them recalled something else pertinent about the assailant. But not now. She set out to beat him solidly this time.

She concentrated on their game for the next hour as the two of them formed words off each other, ate brownies, and chatted about nothing much. Lo and behold, Wanda won by fifty-one points. *Ha!*

As soon as the slightly deflated Todd left, she texted Betty Sue, asking to meet her for a late lunch at Good

Gravy and then make a trek to the Bird Nest. Perhaps one of the ladies would open up a bit more about their experience now that the shock had worn off. People always seemed more at ease and talkative around Betty Sue.

Gluten-Free Blonde Brownies

Ingredients:

- ½ c. salted butter (organic if possible)
- ¾ c. monk fruit or erythritol
- 1 tsp vanilla extract, Mexican vanilla if possible. It tastes so much richer.
- 1 large egg, whisked
- ½ tsp baking powder
- 1 ½ c. almond flour
- ¼ tsp sea salt
- ¾ c. Lucy's sugar free dark chocolate chips

Directions:

1. Preheat oven to 350° F.
2. Microwave the butter in a glass mixing bowl for 20-30 seconds to melt it, but not to reach boiling temperatures. Add in the sweetener and vanilla, then the whisked egg. Mix well until blended.

3. Mix the three dry ingredients together and add slowly, a half a cup at a time to the liquids to make a batter. Whip with a fork to eliminate as many of the lumps as possible.

4. Fold in the chocolate chips evenly then pour the batter into a greased, rectangular pan. Smooth evenly into the corners with a spatula.

5. Bake for 20-25 minutes or until a toothpick comes out clean when inserted in the center.

6. Cool for 30 minutes then cut into squares.

Makes 12-15 brownies, depending on the size. These are not only great for women watching their waists but as afternoon snacks for kids without wiring them up on sugar.

CHAPTER II

Wanda scurried to keep up with her friend's strides as they hoofed it downtown, which added up to a tad more than a mile away. Walking around town, instead of driving like a lot of Texans did, not only gave them good exercise but it had also contributed to their weight loss. She told Betty Sue about Todd's comments. "What if we got Anne and Gloria together to compare notes?"

Betty Sue stopped and took a breath. "I see. It might help them each recall something they may not have thought of before."

"Exactly. But their business hours are totally different. Anne's restaurant doesn't open until eleven and goes until nine at night. Gloria's shop opens at nine and closes at six."

"How will that work then?"

"I figure midafternoon might offer a lull in business

for them both."

Betty Sue's gleam told Wanda she'd caught on. "And you want us to introduce them to ease their minds. That's why we are eating there this late."

"Since their establishments are less than a block apart, maybe Anne could drop by Gloria's for a few minutes around two or so. Doesn't hurt to ask, right?"

"Let's do it then. My afternoon is free."

Wanda side-hugged her friend and they continued their walk. They reminisced about some of the schemes they had implemented over the half century-plus of friendship. Most had turned out well, though a few . . .

Anne greeted them as they entered. She nodded to the waitress also heading in their direction. "It's okay, Ruth. I can seat these two." Then she turned her attention to Wanda and Betty Sue. "Something tells me you are not just here for lunch, correct?"

Wanda felt the hot and cold sensation spread across her cheeks. "We don't mean to pry, but I had an idea. Neither you nor Gloria gave a detailed description of your assailants, except that they both wore turquoise-soled tennis shoes. We thought," she pointed at Betty Sue and herself, "that if you two chatted, it might spark a memory now that the initial shock has worn off."

Anne led them to a table for two. "It is an idea, I guess. In fact, when the police told me what happened to Mrs. Longoria, I wanted to chat with her. But I thought it might be intrusive."

She stared into space for a minute as if pondering the idea. Wanda waited.

Then the woman's eyes widened as they fell back on her two now seated guests. "Things quiet down here in about an hour. Ruby could probably handle the place for a while." She smiled. "Tell you what. I will call Gloria Longoria and see if she wants to join you two for coffee and dessert in an hour or if she'd prefer us to come there."

"Perfect." Maybe then the Bird Nest owner would erase any suspicion about Wanda from the corners of her mind. Wanda scooted her chair forward. "And I don't need a menu. I have been thinking about your blackened chicken salad for days."

Betty Sue ordered the same.

A little after two, Anne, Wanda, and Betty Sue traipsed to Gloria's Bird Nest with a basket of gingerbread slices and mango iced teas in hand. Gloria greeted them and motioned them toward the back into a small kitchenette and office.

To Wanda's surprise, the two lady proprietors hugged.

Betty Sue whispered near Wanda's ear as she took it upon herself to set out the dessert and drinks. "Guess mutual experiences have a way of bonding strangers."

"I have been meaning to come by and greet you but starting up the restaurant has had me in a tailspin." Anne handed Gloria a paper plate containing a slice of gingerbread dribbled with lemon sauce.

"I hear you. Same with me. There is so much to do, even after we close. Balancing the receipts, inventory, sweeping, and cleaning . . ."

The two ladies groaned in unison then laughed.

Gloria's eyes widened at the first bite. "Scrumptious." Then her expression became serious. "Do y'all think we were targeted because we are brand new businesses? Would someone have a grudge or not want us to succeed?"

Wanda had never considered that angle. "I can't imagine any of our merchants in Scrub Oak acting like that. Perhaps your attacker figured you'd be most vulnerable since you don't know very many people."

Anne scrunched her mouth to one side. "Maybe."

"Besides, my neighborhood watch volunteers and the police have been on the lookout for anyone with turquoise-soled sneakers and no one fits the bill. My nephew Todd, who is on the police force, even asked the coaches at the schools and they knew of no one who might own a pair."

"For a good reason." Betty Sue put the back of her hand to her mouth and whispered. "Our biggest rival's colors are turquoise and black."

Both merchants' mouths formed an "o".

Gloria thought for a minute. "The tennis shoes were whiteish. Only the undersoles were turquoise. And I think they were wearing tight, faded jeans, torn at the knees. Yes. And no socks."

Anne sat forward and snapped her fingers. "Mine wore a T-shirt with black and white striped sleeves but had on similar jeans."

"Mine wore a leopard patterned one. And a ski mask."

Anne nodded rapidly. "Yes, red with white deer. Dark bangs peeked out."

"Oh? Mine wore a solid black mask except for a white trim. Didn't notice the color of the hair." Gloria's demeanor deflated like a two-day old helium balloon.

"Okay, the perp had two ski masks. That could mean something." Wanda tried to make her voice sound upbeat. "Maybe they ski in Colorado. Have family there."

Gloria stood and clasped her hand over her heart. "Sweet, Lord Jesus, thank you for your guidance. I remember now. It was a girl."

"A girl?" Wanda and Betty Sue chimed in together.

"Yes, you're right, Gloria." Anne clapped her hands together. "Tall though. And muscular. She had very shapely legs in those skinny jeans. Wait." She stopped and stared into space. "I recall smelling—"

They viewed each other and spoke at the same time. "—Gardenias."

Betty Sue gasped. "Splash Spa in the mall out on the highway has a new line of products they're promoting. I saw it in their display window. Gardenia Glam." She rummaged through her purse. "In fact, I have a sample." She pulled out a postcard with a scratch and sniff feature.

Both business owners took a whiff and nodded.

"Now we're getting somewhere." Wanda pulled her phone out to call Todd.

Anne and Gloria glanced at each other as their shoulders relaxed and the stress of their assaults visibly melted from their faces.

CHAPTER 12

Wanda could detect the frustration in her nephew's voice. "I appreciate you're wanting to help, honestly. But this complicates things."

"How?" In her mind it cleared a lot up. They were now looking for a tall, athletic woman that wore Gardenia Glam and turquoise-soled tennis shoes, who possibly liked to snow ski or snow board, and might have family in Colorado.

"Because Ms. Graves and Ms. Lozano have collaborated, it may have contaminated their true memories. The desire to find their assailant may very well have skewed their recollections."

She turned her back on the others and slipped through to the retail portion of the Bird Nest. "Let me understand. You're saying their minds are filling in the blanks that may not really be there?"

"Exactly. Studies have shown that witnesses see and hear different things but if you put them together in a room long enough, they will all come out with the same identical story. Which is why we rarely question people together."

"Oh." She rubbed her forehead. "But one of them must have smelled gardenias."

"That place in the mall mailed out thousands of those postcards to introduce their new line. Lots of folks have purchased the fragrance. It has actually become one of their top sellers."

"How do you know that, Todd?" Her heart fluttered. Had he bought Rebecca some? Had their relationship developed that far?

"We already checked it out. Reagan noticed the perfume when we entered the Bird Nest because it was so out of character of a pet supply place to smell like flowers. She had gotten the postcard herself, scratched it, and decided it wasn't right for her. So immediately she identified the aroma as being Gardenia Glam."

"I see." She knew disappointment resonated in her response.

"Besides, initial impressions are often not reliable. Recall what Evelyn's was when she was attacked?"

"That's true."

"Sorry, Aunt Wanda. It isn't the lead you'd hoped it to be. Truth is, the perp may have had one of the samples in his or her pocket or be living with someone who had purchased some, or even brushed up against someone on the bus. It's pretty potent smelling stuff."

Defeated, Wanda said goodbye and slipped in the backroom again. Three pair of eager eyes greeted her. Then one by one, their faces drooped.

"Well, the police already knew about the perfume." She told the ladies what Todd said and why identifying the fragrance didn't help very much.

"But surely now that we're both positive it was a woman narrows things down a bit. I mean, how many tall, muscular females live in this town?" Anne drew her eyebrows together.

"I can think of a few in my Zumba class." Betty Sue sighed and rested her chin in her hands. "If Todd wants their names, I'm sure Zelda would cooperate."

Wanda thanked them all. "You never know. It may lead to something. If either of you two recalls anything else, notify Todd or Jimmy Bob at the station."

Gloria and Anne agreed. They said their formalities as people who have just met do when leaving and went back to running their businesses.

Betty Sue and Wanda walked toward home in silence. When they reached the park, Wanda crossed into it to sit on one of the benches. Betty Sue joined her and patted her arm the way Betty Sue often did when sympathizing with someone.

"I honestly thought we were onto something." Wanda

explained what Todd had said about collaborations being a mistake. Then she sighed as she observed the cerulean sky with cotton ball clouds floating over the treetops.

"You always mean well, dear. I know that. So does Todd. Perhaps this one is best left to the police to investigate."

Wanda rolled her eyes, expressing the frustration with herself more than anything. "You're right. I have meddled once again. When will I learn?"

Betty Sue stood and extended her hand to help her friend rise. "Let's go. At least we had a great lunch and some exercise walking around. And got to know two new members of our community a bit better."

Leave it to Betty Sue to put a positive spin on things. Wanda squeezed her best friend's hand in thanks. Then she let go and waved as she diagonally crossed the street to her home.

Once inside, she gave Sophie a treat then sat with a pad and pen at the kitchen table writing down everything she'd heard so far. She tore off the sheet and then wrote the answers to the Hangman puzzle. *Alley*, *nest*. Quite common words. Exactly why she'd chosen them for the first puzzle. First graders could solve them.

Tomorrow's answer would be easy as well. A baby who hoots. *Owlet*, of course, setting *O* as the first word in *oven*, the main answer. Not rocket science by any means. Nor sinister. Simply an innocent game designed to encourage family fun. Who could see the harm in that for heaven's sake?

She crumpled both pages and tossed them toward the trash can in the corner.

Coincidence. Nothing more.

Julie B Cosgrove

CHAPTER 13

Wanda tossed and turned most of the night. In her dream she became surrounded by crowds of faceless females, each reeking of gardenias. They sat around her in the church pews fanning themselves with bulletins featuring the floral scratch and sniff, then several squeezed the oranges in the Grocery Mart that emitted a spritz of gardenia perfume. While a group ordered the gardenia special with fries at Better Burger even more sprayed it on themselves after Zumba class.

She threw her pillow over her face and scrunched further down in the covers.

The next thing she knew her senses jostled to a loud banging on her backdoor. What in the world? She glanced at her alarm clock. It was half past eight already.

In a groggy fog, she slipped on her robe and patted down the hallway. "I'm coming. I'm coming."

Had she forgotten an appointment with some repair person? Not that she recalled. As she entered the kitchen, she saw Todd's face peering in through the glass in the backdoor. He didn't appear happy.

"Todd?" She rubbed her eyes as she let him inside. What was he doing up and in uniform at this hour?

He eyed her up and down. "Woke you, then? Guess you don't know, do you?"

"Know what?" The question became muddled in the middle of her yawn as she poured kibbles into Sophie's bowl to stop the dog's wagging tail from pounding on the floor.

"Someone broke into The Hoot and Owl about an hour ago. Smashed in the backdoor, set off the alarm. Ray jumped up to see what happened, and they whacked him with a champagne bottle. Stole last night's proceeds."

"Is Ray all right?"

"Well, yes and no. He got a good bonk on the head and is a bit shaken, but he is back at work trying to assess the damage." Todd scratched the back of his neck. "Just left from there after the County forensics finished doing their thing."

"Any fingerprints?"

"Nope." He slapped the Friday edition of the newspaper down, folded to the word puzzles. The Words-in-Word glared back at her. From the list she'd given Mason to use for the Words-in-Word, Vicki had chosen the word *restaurant*. And the third Hangman clue of course was *owlet*. Who could have guessed the two would be associated somehow?

"Oh, dear." Her knees buckled as she grabbed for a kitchen chair and slunk into it.

Todd locked his elbows as he leaned his arms on the table and bent to glare into her face. "I gather you have no idea why this is happening?"

"Why would I?" She gulped, but her mouth felt as dry as the Mojave Desert in summer. If only her legs would stop acting like gelatin. Then she might be able to rise and get a glass of water.

"Obviously, someone does." He stood and went in the direction of the kitchen sink.

Behind her she heard a cabinet hinge moan, a clink of glass, and the sound of water pouring. A moment later, a half-filled tumbler sat beside her. She willed her throat to accept the liquid. "Thanks."

Todd pulled out a chair, and as he did, the screech of the legs across her tiled floor made her cringe.

"Sorry." He sat down across from her. "Look, this is getting a bit peculiar, agreed?"

She took another gulp and set the tumbler down. "Yes. But by all that is holy, I honestly do not know what's going on. Poor Ray. Such a kind, honest man."

Todd reared back in the chair. His lips pressed together and his expression reminded her of a lion studying its prey. Not a comfortable feeling.

She rose and grabbed her purse off the peg, dug inside for her checkbook, and sat back down. She wet her finger with her tongue and flipped it open to the first blank check. "How much?"

"Excuse me?"

Wanda raised her attention to her nephew's eyes. "How much does Ray estimate he lost."

Todd snatched the checkbook from her. "He hadn't reconciled the receipts yet, but I'm not telling what the initial estimate is. That's police business. I can tell you it was more than usual. A large rehearsal dinner party booked the backroom last night. Ten bridesmaids."

"Land of mercy. Who?" She didn't know of any brides-to-be in Scrub Oak at the moment.

"His cousin's daughter. They all drove down in limos from Arlington. Evidently the bride is his godchild."

Wanda's brain kicked in for the first time that morning. "Then that's the key. Someone knew there'd be a wad of cash in that register. And they knew Ray wouldn't prepare a bank deposit until this morning."

"Good thought. However, even the toddlers in town know Ray never balances the tills until the next morning. Anyone can watch him sitting at one of the tables with his ledger and calculator so the morning sun streaming through the plate glass windows warms his arthritic hands. This is Scrub Oak, for goodness' sake." Todd let out a huge sigh through his nose.

True. Where everyone knows everyone else's patterns. And no one ever had to lock doors . . . until recently. The fact Ray O'Malley had installed an alarm surprised her. Not many of the merchants had.

Todd rose and put a pod in the coffee machine. Soon the aroma of caffeine whiffed through the room as the soft gurgles and groans of brewing drowned out the mockingbird's repertoire outside in the backyard. Wanda hoped the coffee would be for her. She didn't dare ask considering her nephew's mood.

He set it down along with a packet of stevia, a spoon, and the carton of creamer from the fridge.

Good boy. She smiled a thank you.

He grunted what sounded close to a you're welcome and then made himself a cup.

As he did, he spoke again. "Ray's talked about the wedding for weeks. I'm surprised you didn't know about him hosting the rehearsal dinner last night."

"He and I aren't that close." She stirred some sweetener into her mug. "He goes to Evelyn's church. She probably knew."

"Hmmm." He took his cup and sat back down.

She realized then his uniform appeared crumpled. Had he not slept at all? "Todd, why are you here?"

"Chief wants me to question you then Mason and Vicki. Burglaries have occurred each time the word games have been published in *The Gazette*, and each time . . ."

"The locations coordinated with the clues. I get it." A vice grip began to twist against her temples. She shook it off. "Sorry, I didn't mean to be so abrupt. But this makes me angry."

His expressionless gaze didn't change.

Wanda slammed her mug to the table, spilling a splotch onto her cloth. "Dagnabbit! We designed these to bring families back together, and some idiot has spoiled it." Heat penetrated the back of her eyes and she sniffled through the burning in her nostrils.

Todd grabbed a paper towel and mopped up the spill. Then he took her hands in his. "Aunt Wanda. Listen to me. Who else would know in advance what the word puzzles would be?"

"Me, Vicki maybe, and of course Mason since he has to digitize them or whatever. He and Vicki also decided which of the ones I wrote out to use in the Words-In-Word."

"Interesting." He released her fingers, took out his black-covered note pad, and jotted in it. "No one else?"

She shook her head. "Not that I'm aware."

"Then one of you three is feeding information to a burglar. I don't want to think it's you."

"Why would you think it's any of us?"

"Because all three incidences occurred within an hour or so of when the newspaper hit the stands, so to speak. Of course, the online versions all were emailed at seven in the morning."

"So, then someone with internet access solved the puzzles early in the morning and decided who to hit." Wanda splayed her hands on the table.

"Doubtful. No fingerprints were left behind, so he or she wore gloves. He or she knew the tills would be full. These robberies appear to be planned out, as most are. Not spontaneous as if the puzzles helped them decide who to hit."

"How long does it take to grab gloves?" She waggled a finger at him. "Pardon me for saying so, but these three all seem like hit and runs, no pun intended. My guess is the burglar lives elsewhere."

"I hope you're right. Vicki is an old friend. And Mason seems like a great guy." He leaned in and brushed her cheek with his lips. "And I'm rather fond of my aunt as well. I don't want to see any of you handcuffed."

He got up and left her kitchen.

Wanda stared as he closed the door behind him. Did he seriously think she might be involved? Surely not.

For a moment Wanda thought of packing a bag and visiting her son B.J. It had been a while since she'd seen the grandkids. Would the police think she had skedaddled to avoid arrest and put out an All-Points Bulletin on her?

Images zipped across her imagination—red flashing lights, squawking highway patrol radios, and herself in handcuffs slammed face down against the hood of her car as Sophie whimpered and scratched the windshield.

Oh, get a grip.

CHAPTER 14

Wanda didn't know how long she sat with her coffee mug in her hand staring at the caramel colored liquid. A rappity-rap-rap, Betty Sue's signature knock, sounded on the glass of her backdoor.

Bless that woman. She almost had a sixth sense when someone needed a shoulder to cry upon. And right now, Wanda felt like throwing adult dignity aside and doing just that. She swiped her lowered eyelids and answered the door.

The expression on her almost life-long friend told Wanda she had seen the morning paper already. She beckoned Betty Sue inside. "Yeah, I heard. Todd just left."

"I know. Evelyn saw him drive away in his cruiser as she left for her annual mammogram in Fort Worth. She knew something must be wrong so she texted me."

Warmth covered Wanda's heart. Big city folk might

consider it an intrusion of privacy but to her it oozed of small town camaraderie. "Then you don't know." Her voice cracked.

Betty Sue guided her back to the kitchen table. "Tell me."

Wanda relayed the latest events, and surprisingly held her emotions in check as she did.

"You didn't know Mason would choose *restaurant* as the Words-in-Word?"

"Nope. I knew the Hangman word he'd be using, but he let Vicki choose the Words-in-Word. But it seems someone else did know." Hearing the words coming from her own voice sent a sinking feeling through her system. She leaned back in the chair and sighed.

Betty Sue scrunched her mouth to the side, an expression that meant her brain wheels spun.

Wanda let her friend ponder as she rose and heated up her mug in the microwave. "Want any coffee or tea?"

Betty Sue shook her head. That's when Wanda noticed her new hairdo.

"When did you get your hair cut?"

"Last Tuesday, but I understood why you didn't notice. Fred did, though. Said he thought it very becoming."

"Oh, when was this?'

"Last night." She blushed. "We went to dinner and a play in Cleburne."

"Nice." They had been seeing a great deal of each other the past few months. That pleased Wanda. They made a cute couple, both being widowed, and Betty Sue was the type who needed a man in her life. Wanda slipped into the kitchen chair opposite her friend and sipped the coffee. Ouch, too hot. It burned her tongue. She fanned her mouth and rose to get an ice cube from the freezer.

Betty Sue pouted in sympathy. "This really has you in a tizzy doesn't it?"

"Yeth." She dabbed the cube on the tip of her tongue for a minute then set it in the spoon next to her coffee. "Gloria almost accused me of plotting this."

"She did?"

"Well, she hinted at it anyway. To the police. Thought I might have an ulterior motive for visiting, like I was casing the joint." She stopped, noticed Betty Sue's eyebrows rise, and smirked. "I know. But hey, she didn't know me from Adam, or should I say Eve? Anyway, when we met with her and Anne, she seemed to have warmed a bit."

"You are concerned that if she jumped to that conclusion, others will as well?"

Wanda bobbed her head as a tear escaped. Darn it. She brushed it off her cheek and bent to scratch Sophie's floppy ear.

Betty Sue pressed her hand to Wanda's arm. "Don't let the devil steal your joy. You have done a lot for this community in the past two years. No one is going to think that."

"I sure hope not. Though Todd's face showed concern when he dropped by." She managed a half smile. "Thanks for coming over, and for being my friend."

Betty Sue sniffled and side hugged her. "I have to go meet Fred. He wants my opinion on picking out dishes."

"I see. Choosing patterns already?"

"Stop. For his granddaughter. Getting her first apartment." Her apple cheeks reddened. "I am a phone call away if you need me, though. Always."

Wanda waved as the door closed. Her shoulders relaxed for the first time that morning. No one could possibly accuse her or the Clyburns of any of this. Despite the recent history of crime solving on her part, this time word games did not enter into the equation. No way.

Okay, maybe subconsciously Vicki picked the word *restaurant* because the Hangman clue was an *owlet*. Hook & Owl probably sat on the front of her brain anyway because the newspaper no doubt would cover the reception. Simple enough. It didn't make her or Mason a mastermind thief. This wasn't some TV movie plot.

Just because Wanda had not known about the reception didn't mean half the town hadn't. Her mind had been preoccupied. She texted Hazel. *Did you know about Ray's niece getting married?*

The response came back in seconds. Hazel must have

had her phone nearby. *"Sure. They wanted red roses and Kay asked if I could supply a few for the bouquet. Seems her shipment got lost."*

She texted two other friends. They each knew as well. There. Proof enough. Someone told someone who mentioned it to another person and slowly the word found the ears of a less reputable individual. Or maybe the wedding coordinator had a relative with sticky fingers. Who knew? Maybe a passerby saw the full parking lot and got ideas.

She drained her coffee cup and headed down the hall to shower and dress for the day, her footsteps considerably lighter. As she shampooed her hair, she went over the puzzle clues in her head. Number six would be published next.

Scrub Oak didn't have a jewelry store so the next clue, "a piece of jewelry around the throat" shouldn't be an issue at all, right? Next Tuesday would be quiet and peaceful. Then they'd see.

She dried and styled her hair, slipped on some denim capris with a T-shirt from a past women's church retreat, then scrambled some eggs. As she munched her breakfast she flipped to the front headlines of *The Gazette.*

She almost dropped her fork.

Gazette Accused of Involvement in Recent Robberies. The byline read: by Editor in Chief, Mason Clyburn.

Wanda groaned. "Mason, what have you done?"

Julie B Cosgrove

CHAPTER 15

Wanda grabbed her purse and keys and drove way above the speed limit to the newspaper office. She pushed open the door with such force, all the color left Vicki's face.

Not good to scare a woman two weeks from labor. She stopped, took a long inhale, and pumped her hands. "It's all right. May I speak with Mason?"

Vicki ducked her eyes. "Not here. Mayor Arnold called him to his office. Supposedly the article on the front page is not making the Chamber of Commerce happy. Several members have contacted him."

Wanda plopped into a side chair. "I should say not. I know Mason is gung-ho on selling papers, but . . ."

Vicki winced and rubbed her tummy, then took in a long, cleansing breath.

Wanda's heart jerked. "You okay?"

The pregnant woman nodded. "Ian is getting highly active. I think he will end up with a soccer scholarship one day." She gave off a small grin and took another breath. "It seems everyone read the headline but not the article—you included?"

"Guilty. I guess I should."

Vicki handed her a copy. The article went on to state that *The Gazette* took no responsibility whatsoever and that the robberies were purely coincidental. It ended with a quote from Todd:

> Our police force is looking into several leads, one of which is that someone hacked into *The Gazette's* database ahead of time and knew what the puzzle answers would be. The Clyburns, who are now in charge of the local newspaper's day-to-day operations, have been cooperating with us to track any suspicious cyberspace activity.

Wanda glanced up from the newsprint. "I didn't know. I'm sorry."

Vicki gave her head a small bob and increased her smile. Ian had obviously resettled in the womb. "Mason knew there were risks in going digital, but it never occurred to us that we'd have hackers so soon. For us it's the only explanation."

Wanda whispered a thank you but Vicki's reference to her unsaid accusation still pierced her heart. She shifted her eyes to scan the rest of the newspaper. Another article followed on page two about how people can better protect their computers. Mason had interviewed a computer science professor at Texas Christian University in Fort Worth.

"Very well written." She pointed at it. "Who is Jake Overby, the author?"

"A journalism student in his junior year at TCU. He will be coming onboard as an intern this summer. You'll meet him next week."

If Wanda could have slid back under the door and onto the sidewalk welcome mat, she would have attempted it. Hadn't lost that much weight though. "Look, Vicki, I'm—"

The woman waved her hand to erase the thought. "—It's all right, Wanda. There, see? I called you by the right name."

That made Wanda grin. Tom and Misty had raised a fine daughter. She had known Vicki through Todd in high school and at the time thought she had a bit of a snarky streak, bordering on defiant. But no one ever really got to know teens, did they? And college either makes them or breaks them. Vicki definitely adored her dad and worked hard at the paper. Wanda had begun to see what an amazing young woman sat in front of her.

"You're going to be a wonderful mom, by the way."

Vicki's face warmed. "Aw, thanks. I am so very nervous."

"Everyone is. You don't have to know everything on day one. Parenthood grows with the child."

The young woman's face glowed even more. "Would you consider doing an article on that? I think it would make a wonderful entry. 'Ten things every new parent should not worry about.'" She mimed the headline in space with her hand.

Wanda lost her train of thought. "Well . . . I . . . I mean . . ."

"Of course, Mason will have the final say, but if you could type it up by Monday, say five hundred to six hundred words?"

Wanda pressed her lips into a line. Now she'd be an occasional reporter? Could God grace her any more than that? She swallowed. "Sure. All right. Do I print it out and bring it in or email it?'

"Email is fine. Easier to edit."

Wanda rose and almost tripped on her own sandals. "Thanks. And again, I am sorry I flew off the handle."

"No worries. This has us all on edge."

The door opened to Kay dropping off her latest floral advertisement for the next edition. Wanda bid her hello and exited into the sunshiny spring day, a lilt in her step. She decided to go next door to Sally's and get a blueberry muffin, with a pat of real butter. Maybe two. With a glass of freshly squeezed cherry limeade. Then she'd drive home.

She took four steps and halted. Wait a minute.

Awfully slick how Vicki smoothed her ruffled feathers. No doubt Mason did the same thing with the mayor right now. She glanced up at the building in town square housing the mayor's chambers.

Had she just been bamboozled? Had the mayor?

Julie B Cosgrove

CHAPTER 16

Wanda lost her appetite for the muffin. She wanted to replay in her head in slo-mo all that happened, if possible. Analyze facial expressions, nuances, anything that might clue her into what occurred. Not that she didn't trust Vicki. She had no solid reason to *not* believe her. But somehow, someway, someone had gained access to their word puzzles. Were Wanda and the Clyburns simply pawns in an elaborate hacker game?

She strutted to her car and slid inside, her hands on the steering wheel. She stared into space as if it held the answer. *Holy Spirit, I could use your discernment right about now.*

If Vicki, and perhaps Mason, were conning half the town then why involve her? Had they offered her the word puzzle contributions as a cover-up? No, no, no. They would have had no idea as to what she would have come up with ahead of time. Unless . . .

Did they read her entries and then come up with a scheme? To what end? They had good jobs. Okay, they were practically newlyweds with a baby on the way. Did they have insurance? Babies were expensive. Plus, they had just bought a house on Mesquite and 5th Street. An older section of town, the houses were prime real estate for the open concept generation who wanted to gut bungalows. Maybe it became a money pit?

She slammed the palm of her hand onto the steering wheel. Ridiculous. Grabbing at straws for heaven's sake. How could she suspect two people helping her fulfill an unspoken dream, one she had never declared to Betty Sue, Evelyn, or even to Todd? No, a hacker seemed far more likely.

In her imagination, Wanda pictured a lone failure-to-launch twenty-something in his—or her—childhood room with four computer screens, along with pizza boxes and drink containers strewn amongst dirty socks and geek paraphernalia. Alone in the house while the parents slaved at jobs to support her or his habit, all the while not knowing their darling daughter or son had thousands stored up by informing gangs on who to rob when.

One of the neighborhood watch folks read that these techies could hack into bank systems and turn ATM cameras around to watch password inputs. Trouble was, Scrub Oak had only one ATM—at the bank's drive-through. Except for the convenience store near the Woodway Resort on the lake.

Argghhh. She threw her head back and bonked her skull on the headrest. That hurt. Now she needed ibuprofen. With a long, arduous sigh, she keyed the ignition and drove home at a more normal, legal snail pace.

Thunder rumbled and the sky darkened. In a few seconds later, a second roll brought sheets of spring rain pelting her windshield. Great, just great. And the battery in her garage door opener had died last week. On her list of things to do. *Could this day get any worse, Lord?*

Her dashboard read 11:02 AM. Maybe she'd crawl back into bed for the rest of the day and hope tomorrow would be better.

Wrong attitude. If Wanda allowed herself a pity party for too long, others might want to invite themselves in and make things worse. No, the best way to solve this crime spree lay in finding the turquoise-soled soul who caused such havoc in her community. If she had to hire a hound dog to sniff out Gardenia Glam on each stranger in the nearby towns, she would.

Then it hit her, as things often do. This perp, she—or he—had to get away each time. Running would only get them so far. That meant a vehicle. She had to speak with Anne and Gloria again, this time separately. And talk with Ray as well.

Did any of them recall hearing an engine? Did they smell diesel or gasoline? See something out of the corner of their eyes?

Wanda turned her car around at the park and went back toward downtown. Gloria and Ray had both been attacked in their establishments. Anne outside. She'd start with her.

She, Mason, and Vicki were victims just as much as the proprietors who had been robbed. By golly, Scrub Oak's reputation didn't serve to be violated like this, not by anyone. Cyber punk or not.

CHAPTER 17

Wisdom kicked in, or perhaps common sense. Wanda decided to not barge unexpectedly into Good Gravy for a third time. No, she had to plan the meeting out. She turned around again and headed back as the rain gave her a free carwash. Storm clouds often moved fast and furious in Texas during the spring. Thank goodness it rang true this time and had slowed to a trickle by the time she entered her driveway.

When she got inside, she pulled up the restaurant's website, clicked the contact button, and sent Anne an email asking her when they could get together. Next, she did the same for Gloria. Wanda explained that she was in the process of drafting gift donation agreements so they were official, for tax purposes. Not a falsehood, she had thought about it and planned to run it by Mason.

She also had half-way developed a newcomer's

brochure to be put out by the neighborhood watch teams and wanted Anne's and Gloria's opinions on it as newcomers. May as well ask Ray for his opinion too as an established owner in town. She searched his site and then cut and pasted her message into his contact form.

It would be easy to segue into a discussion of security and then talk about their experiences. Then another idea struck her. A survey!

She poured herself some iced tea, gave Sophie a doggie biscuit, and peered at the computer screen. She quickly found a template and began to fill in the blanks. Title: How Can We Make Downtown Safer? She added the Neighborhood Watch logo centered in the header for authenticity and wrote under it The City of Scrub Oak, Texas. Five quick generalized questions with plenty of space for her merchants to write their responses filled the front and back of a single sheet of copy paper. Not bad.

Wanda decided to print off ten copies. That many surveys would make a good representation in a town of their size. She'd give five to Evelyn so she could hand them out to each of the five watch folk in the downtown sector as her first official act as captain. She added instructions asking each of them to pick a business, set up a time with the merchant or owner to go over the survey, and then bring the answers to the next neighborhood watch meeting. That would give them several days to complete her request. Should be plenty of time.

She picked Sally's Salads and Beverly Newby from Anna's Antiques to interview herself since they were women merchants, along with interviewing the victims Anne, Gloria, and Ray. She felt she owed them that much. Wanda sat back, pleased with herself for coming up with this plan. *It's okay to feel a bit bubbly over a brilliant idea, right, Lord?*

Pride opened the door to sin, as her pastor had stated in his sermon last Sunday, but she never intended to step over the stoop.

As if her mental radar had tuned in, Betty Sue phoned. Wanda told her of the idea.

"I think that is a wonderful plan. Proactive. In fact, I'm very proud of you taking this appointment as chairperson of the neighborhood watch so seriously. No one can say you are not doing a great job and are the right woman to lead it."

Wanda stammered. Alone in her kitchen, she knew her face appeared as red as the delicious apples in her fruit bowl. "Well, to be honest, Betty Sue I wanted a legitimate way to interview Anne Graves, Gloria Longoria, and Ray O'Malley about their experiences and the rest floated together like alphabet letters forming a word in a soup bowl. That's not wrong, is it?"

"No dear. Just be careful. You don't want to get on Todd's bad side."

"Right. Exactly. Did you know he half suspected me

or Vicki or Mason of somehow being involved?"

"What?" Her answer came out in such a high-pitched screech, Wanda pulled the cell phone from her left ear.

"He is just doing his job, following every possible scenario. Analyzing, you know. I get that." She sighed and took a long gulp of her tea. "In fact, I had an inkling of a doubt myself about Mason and Vicki."

"Wanda, no."

"Well, think about it. Someone informed this thief ahead of time. And Mason did say it would be good publicity for the paper if a mystery shrouded it. Plus, a little while ago when I confronted Vicki about today's headlines, she diverted the conversation to me writing an article on advice for new parents."

"Do you hear yourself?" Betty Sue's voice took on that teacher tone again.

"Yeah, I know." Wanda slumped in her chair as if she'd been caught making spit wads in class. "Never mind. Talk to me about something else."

"Well, Henrietta emailed me a copy of her sonogram. Another boy. Due in October."

"Wonderful. That makes four grandkids, doesn't it? Two for her, and two for Beatrice."

"Yep. I have almost given up on Susie. Married to her career."

"I hear you. I feel the same about my daughter, except she had never had a career."

Betty Sue sighed. "Different drummers."

"Yes."

Wanda's mind wandered to the burglar. A muscular female? One who could lift a twenty-five pound bag of bird seed and make it a weapon, whack someone in the head with a trash can lid like Wonder Woman and burst through a metal door. Different drummer indeed. Why had she not thought of that before?

She needed to ask Coach Micky Lozano about the plausibility.

Of course, getting in touch with a coach on a Friday afternoon is like catching a pastor on Sunday morning for a lengthy theological discussion ten minutes before the service began—not exactly opportune timing. Perhaps next Wednesday would be a low time for him since the students would be knee-deep in taking their year-end finals. Wanda added a tickler in her phone calendar to call him midday on Monday and set up a little chat.

Wanda glanced at the calendar's entries. This afternoon she had agreed to fold and distribute fliers in her neighborhood for her church's May Fest activities. Hazel invited her to tea at four so she could bounce off new ideas for her back flower beds. Evelyn invited her to the Hook and Owl Saturday afternoon for a fundraiser to help Ray recover his losses. Wanda reluctantly agreed to attend. Sunday would involve church services, of course, then a final planning meeting after lunch for the May Fest decorating committee, which would then meet on the next Saturday afternoon after the women's luncheon, to set up the fellowship hall and grounds.

Note to self, finish ironing the tablecloths.

Sheesh. Plus, she had agreed, she guessed, to write that new parenting article before Monday as well. Then there was the laundry, which she had put off for the second week in a row. She had one pair of clean undies left, so she had better make that a priority. Adding the chore to the list, Wanda felt a tad overwhelmed. Who said retirees lead a lazy, relaxed life? She never felt this busy while raising two kids and holding down a job.

Shoveling in a quick bacon, lettuce, and Gouda cheese sandwich on multigrain forty-five calorie bread, Wanda bid Sophie farewell and headed for the church to fold fliers. When she walked in the double doors to the fellowship hall, the buzz of voices stopped. Her heart bounced into the sandwich in her stomach. She cleared her throat and entered the room.

"Wanda, we were just discussing the recent crime wave." Emma Jean put her hand on her ample chest. "Scary. What is happening to our dear town?"

The room became so quiet a mouse chomping cheese in the wall would have sounded like a bulldozer revving up. Wanda's eyes traveled to the twelve pair staring back at her, waiting for a response. Did they seek her out as chairperson of the neighborhood watch or as the clue giver of the newspaper whose word puzzles debut happened to coincide with the robberies?

"I know the police are investigating every angle. I am in the process of developing a brochure for newcomers, residential and commercial, so they will learn who their neighborhood watch people are and how to reach them. Plus, we plan to survey our downtown business owners this week on how we can better serve them in keeping their establishments safe from crime."

A few heads bobbed as they turned to glance at each other. Several more continued to bore a hole into her as if they expected more. Like what? A full confession? *Yes, I deviously planned this whole thing to destroy my reputation and go to jail.* Sheesh.

"So . . ." She clapped her hands and rubbed them together. "Who needs me to fold fliers?"

Over the next hour, everyone occupied themselves with the task. Even so, Wanda's back felt as if several eyes continued to land on her. She swallowed down the hurt that began to rise. She'd gone to church with many of these people most of her life. Didn't they know her by now? This should be a sanctuary of support and prayer.

Wanda's eyes caught her pastor walking down the hallway to his office. She excused herself and went to stop him. She needed advice, perhaps absolution, though for what she had not a clue.

"Pastor Bob?'

"Wanda." He halted and then dropped his head to peer at her over his reading glasses. "Is everything all right?"

"No." It came out in a sob.

He ushered her into his office, quietly closed the door, and then took her hands to pray.

For the next hour she regurgitated everything. He sat quietly, listening, with his fingers tented in front of his face, asking questions only to clarify that he understood correctly.

"Well?" She took in a deep breath, which relieved the pressure on her chest.

His executive chair creaked as he eased forward. "Well . . ." He wrapped his hands through each other across his desk. The wrinkles on his forehead told her he deeply thought about all she had relayed to him. Wanda trusted him completely to give her good advice so she remained silent while he pondered his response.

"It is certainly a condition of the human mind to try to fill in the blanks any way it can as quickly as it can. And that is where our skewed reasoning comes into play. Instead of waiting on the right answers to materialize, we speculate." Pastor Bob gave Wanda a small grin. "We all do it."

"True." The cinch around her chest began to loosen further.

"Our laws tell us a person is innocent until proven guilty, but more and more our society seems to want to reverse that process. Especially the media."

"You mean *The Gazette*?"

He pushed his lower lip forward and shook his head. "No, no. Though I'm not sure of the prudency to publish that article. Mason is young and gung-ho. He wanted his first full edition without Tom's approval to be a smash. He'll learn."

Oh. Wanda had not considered that angle. Of course. Tom and Misty had headed to New York and then out on their cruise.

"No, I mean the mainstream media, conservative and liberal. Sensationalism and opinion has become the substitute for unbiased reporting. We cannot help but be influenced by it. It is everywhere. On our TVs, the car radio, even our emails, and phones." He leaned even closer and whispered to her. "We preachers are not immune, you know. I have heard some doozies on the radio."

"People often jump to conclusions, I guess."

He rose and came around to hike his hip on his desk and peered lovingly into Wanda's eyes like a father would. "Exactly. So, you be careful not to do just that, under any circumstances. Pray for clarity. God will handle the rest."

Blinking new tears from forming, she nodded her head rapidly and rose to shake his hand. "Thanks" was all she managed to whisper. Her admiration for his gift of wisdom renewed and she thanked God for his being her pastor.

Wanda walked back into the fellowship hall, picked up her fifty fliers to distribute, and waved so long to everyone. Let them gossip. The truth would come out . . . eventually. She planned to assist in that process as best she could.

CHAPTER 18

Transparency. That would be the key. With that in mind, she trotted the short distance to the police station and entered.

"Mrs. Warner. Can we help you?" Reagan raised her chin as she cupped the phone receiver pressed to her ear, obviously putting the caller on hold for a moment.

Wanda caught Chief Brooks's large form out of the corner of her eye. At six-five, even with white hair and a moustache, he still oozed a don't-mess-with-Texas authority, especially anyone thinking of messing in his town. She called out his name. The chief halted and turned on his heel toward her.

"Got a minute? I won't be long. Neighborhood watch business."

He motioned with his coffee cup for her to follow him to his office.

She finger-waved to Todd as she passed his office and almost relished in the confused expression on his face.

"Have a seat. What can I do you for?" The chief's Texas drawl and deep bass tone oozed power but the twinkle in his eye made even the toddlers in town look to him like a protective grandad who could slay dragons.

Wanda explained about the survey. "I should have brought you the ones I've printed, sorry. But I have them in a Word app on my phone." She scrolled to the questionnaire and the flier. "Maybe you can view them there?" She held out her phone for him.

He shook his head. Then he raised his voice. "Martin. Got a sec?"

She heard her Todd's rushed footfall. "Sir? Oh, hi, Aunt Wanda."

She smiled up at her nephew.

"Can you get what's on her phone to print out on our copier?"

"I believe so. Yes, sir."

Wanda handed her cell phone to Todd and watched as he punched buttons and swiped his finger. Within a few seconds, the whirr of the office copier sounded in the hallway.

"Good lad. Bring them here so I can look over them. Thanks."

In a few more seconds Todd reentered and laid the printouts on the chief's desk.

He picked them up and studied each page. His white moustache twitched and then a smile emerged. "Very nice. Great idea."

Wanda's face warmed. She glanced at Todd who winked. He'd obviously glanced at them on the way back. Well, she didn't mind. She would have done the same thing. Curiosity must be in their genes.

The chief handed the papers to Todd. Then he leaned forward and pressed the intercom. "Reagan. Go grab Jimmy Bob before he heads out. Tell him to meet us in the conference room. You as well. Put the phones on voice mail."

Wanda turned her attention to Todd for confirmation. Was this happening? To be included in a conference with the chief of police sounded huge.

Her nephew's lips pursed to keep from smirking, but his eyes sparkled with pride, which made her all goosey-bumpy.

The chief stood and offered his hand for Wanda to rise from her chair. She accepted it. He smiled and motioned. "Two doors down on the right. I will be there in a few."

Todd followed her and then scooted past her to open the door and pull out a chair for her. The boy did know his manners. She hoped he did the same for Rebecca whenever . . . *oh, never mind.*

"It seems you are slowly winning over the chief." He chose a chair directly across the table from her. The warmth in her nephew's expression spoke volumes. She had begun to wonder if he doubted her intentions.

The meeting went well and all the police force approved of the idea. Ten minutes later, she floated out of the station, feeling exonerated. With a verbal stamp of approval and a compliment from the chief himself, she stopped by her house to retrieve the other ten fliers and headed to Evelyn's since her friend had fully taken Collin's place as captain of the downtown neighborhood watch sector. Perhaps before the fund raiser for Ray tomorrow, they could do the rounds instead of asking the five volunteers to take time out of their day. That way, though everyone knew Ev, Wanda could officially introduce her.

Then people would see Wanda, as chairperson of the neighborhood watch teams, had their best interests at heart. Any rumors floating around about her involvement in these robberies would be squished like a mosquito on a shirt sleeve.

Evelyn answered her door sporting a nose that would compete with Rudolph the Reindeer. She dabbed it with a tissue. "Yo don't wanna come in." Sniff. "I got a tewible cold."

"Oh, dear. What can I do for you? Do you need any shopping done, or chicken soup?"

Evelyn turned to sneeze then imitated a goose honking as she blew into the tissue. "So dweet of you to ask. I'm otay fo now." She started to close the door but stopped and slumped against the jamb. "No, I'm not."

Wanda helped her to her recliner, brought her a glass of water and a box of Kleenex. Then she draped an afghan over her friend's lap. "Want me to brew some hot tea?"

A puppy-dog plea floated into Evelyn's bloodshot eyes. "Des. Wiff wemon."

"Coming right up." Living next door for more than a decade, Wanda knew Evelyn's kitchen as well as her own. And how she liked her tea. She sliced the tangy fruit into wedges, placed one in a mug and wrapped the others in a bowl. Soon the kettle whistled. She poured the water over the English Breakfast tea bag, Evelyn's favorite brew, and stirred in two teaspoons of raw sugar.

"Here you are." She set the mug on the side table.

Evelyn breathed in the steam as best she could and then closed her eyes and rested her head on the back of the recliner. "Yo a dood fwiend."

"You're a good friend to me, too, my dear. Rest up, and I am a phone call away, all right?"

She sneezed again and gazed at Wanda, her eyes pleading even more. "I hate ta ask."

"Wahcha need?"

"Can you get me cough dwops, tissues, coewd medicine and menthol wub fom Joe's?" That was the pharmacy in town.

"Absolutely. Back in a jiffy. We will settle up later."

Wanda lathered on some hand sanitizer, dropped the fliers back off at her house, then drove to the drug store on the first floor of the medical center to gather the items in her shopping basket. Madge chomped her chewing gum as she rang them up. "Who has a cold?"

"Evelyn Jacobs." She stuck her debit card in the scanner.

"Too bad. Third person today. Take care of yourself." Smack. "Do you want a disposable mask to wear around her? Three for a dollar?" She pointed to the kiosk near the counter.

Wanda declined, then thought again. If a new virus tried to make its way through town, she certainly didn't want it to find her. "Well, okay. Ring it up separately. Cash. Thanks, Marge." The woman had the knack for selling things, that's for sure.

"By the way, not that y'all need to advertise being the only pharmacy in town, but we are putting together a little newcomer packet, and if Joe would like to add some coupons or a free tiny gift certificate, let me know. You have my number."

Marge grinned, showing her gum to be spearmint judging by the almost chartreuse color. "I'll let him know. He's making a delivery right now." Smack. "Alli's out. Cut her hand open on a glass that exploded in the dishwasher this morning." Smack.

Alli, his granddaughter, usually delivered

prescriptions on her bike when she wasn't stocking shelves. An image of Joe with his bald head bent over Alli's handlebars, pharmacy white jacket flapping, as he peddled up Elm flashed through Wanda's brain. She stifled a laugh.

More than likely he took his gray SUV. She waved goodbye and almost bumped into Beverly Newby who owned Anna's Antiques, named after her grandmother. "Oh, my. I was just about to come see you. Will you be back in the store in a while? Neighborhood watch business." She held up her plastic sack. "I need to take these to Evelyn Jacobs first. Bad cold."

Beverly glanced at her watch, a vintage gold-rimmed one on a back elastic band. "How about three o'clock?"

"Great. See you then."

As Wanda clicked the fob to her car she halted as if frozen by a death ray gun. Wait a minute. Wanda stared at the sky for a moment as her thoughts twirled through her brain.

Like Joe, Alli had a tall, lean stature. She'd been a track star in high school and landed a scholarship with the university in Austin if memory served. After living a sheltered life inside a strict fundamentalist family, her freshman year ended in disaster. Drugs, plummeting grades, and a total change in personality. After an explosive row with her parents, Joe had taken her in and given her a job. She's seemed to have straightened up again, but if any female in town could have the strength to weal a large bag of birdseed, she could. Plus, Alli would know many of the merchants' schedules whom she often waved to as she tootled around town. Probably delivered to them on a regular basis since they couldn't leave their stores.

Did she really cut her hand on a drinking glass, or could it have been a champagne bottle as it came down on Ray's head?

Hmmm. Wonder what color of tennies she wore?

CHAPTER 19

Asking the color of someone's athletic shoe wear isn't a common part of conversation, so Wanda decided to not go back into the pharmacy. However, it would be for Coach Lozano. Todd had spoken with him, but she wanted to ask him a few more questions. She texted Betty Sue for his phone number in the teacher directory so she could ask for an appointment for Wednesday. Then she headed back to her street to drop off Evelyn's remedies and grab the folder with the neighborhood fliers.

Even with Evelyn under the weather, Wanda could still let the merchants know about the changing of the guard, so to speak, and tell them Ev would drop by after May Fest to talk with them. Making sure Ev had all she needed, and Sophie, too, Wanda grabbed the fliers and headed to Anna's Antiques. Then she planned to stop off at Sally's and Hardware Haven, and finally zip by A Cut

Above to check on how Rebecca's handled things with Claudia gone. She wanted to spend more time with her anyway since her nephew seemed to be doing the same. Tomorrow she'd go by Thrifty Treasures, Tom Jacob's other enterprise. Then bop over to Bargain Boutique, Kay's Flowers, and the vet's since she needed to get more heartworm prevention chews for Sophie anyway.

The temperatures remained mild because a blanket of dove gray clouds hung overhead to block out the sunrays. The weatherman had guaranteed the rain would not develop until after dark and would not be severe when it did. She hoped so since she decided to walk. Even so she had tucked her collapsible umbrella in her purse. Always a coin toss in Texas to trust the forecast or not.

The bell dinged as she entered the antique shop. It always smelled like her grandmother's home in there. A mixture of Old English polish, lemon oil, and aged wood tickled her nose. Beverly waved as she finished wrapping a treasure for Mrs. Blewitt. Probably more milk glass. The woman collected it.

Wanda waved back and then smiled politely as Mrs. Blewitt exited. They had never been more than acquaintances ever since Sophie got out and dug up her newly planted tulip bulbs ten years ago. Or was it eleven? No matter.

"Hi Wanda. What brings you by today?" Bev undid her apron, thus the reason for the fresh lemon oil aroma.

She'd been dusting and polishing.

"I am making the rounds. Evelyn is taking over for Collin as neighborhood captain for downtown. She'd be here as well but, as I said, she has picked up a cold."

"Oh, my. Going around, I guess. Mrs. Blewitt told me her grandson has an upper respiratory infection, and she is worried he won't do well on his finals next week." She lowered her voice as if someone else could hear. "Trying for a scholarship. Parents can't afford to send him to college."

"Who can these days?" Wanda handed her the flier. "This is a brief questionnaire asking for ways we can help your business be safer. I am doing this with Chief Brooks's stamp of approval after the rash of robberies lately."

Her delicate, blue-veined hand flew to her chest. "I know. To be honest, my heart jumps each time I hear that bell. First time since I took over fifteen years ago that I've felt uneasy unlocking and locking up."

"Exactly what we want to prevent. If our merchants are not comfortable opening their doors, then the community won't be comfortable shopping. This affects the whole town."

"Are the police any closer to discovering who is doing this?"

Wanda glanced down at the counter and shook her head. A glittery something caught her eye. Beneath the glass were several pieces of jewelry. Small, teardrop-shaped earrings set in silver filagree offset by amethysts perched inside a matching necklace. Next to the grouping lay another silver necklace featuring art deco turquoise rays along with dangle earrings in the same design. A choker of soft pink pearls with a lobster clasp sat in the middle.

"When did you start selling jewelry?"

Beverly opened the sliding door on her side and pulled the tray out. "Aren't they amazing? They came by carrier this morning. The amethysts are from around 1928 and the turquoise set is early Art Deco, maybe 1921. The pearls are some of the first cultured ones from Japan. My dealer estimates about 1913."

"The pearls are amazing." Wanda tactfully glanced at the tag on the pearls. $2,999.00. Yipes. Who in Scrub Oak would buy them? "You do have an alarm system, right?"

Beverly blinked. "I never thought of getting one. You think I should?" Her eyes scanned the shop. "I do have some fine pieces. Who should I call?"

What? Oh, my goodness. Wanda let out a small cough. "Ask your son-in-law, Jay. After all, he's your insurance agent."

The woman smiled and pointed a crooked finger at Wanda. "Smart idea. Thank you." Then her smile disappeared. "Oh, dear. He is on vacation until Sunday."

"Maybe his assistant can help then?"

"I'll call and see." She winked. "I appreciate the suggestion."

Wanda bought a package of mints and a copy of *Life* Magazine from January 10, 1955 with Greta Garbo on the cover. Her eldest grandson, Ethan, was into movie stars from that era for some reason. His fourteenth birthday would be next month.

Next, she stopped by Hardware Haven. Henry Hampton greeted her with a wave as he put back some wrenches on hooks in descending order. She told him about the survey and the newcomer program in case he wanted to donate. He did—a calendar like the one Todd had in his office and a 25% off coupon on paint and hardware.

"Oh, guess what? Aurora Stewart's house finally sold." He grinned as he dug out a stack of calendars.

"Really?" Aurora Stewart had been Wanda's nemesis all through school. She'd returned several years ago dripping in diamonds courtesy of her third—or was it fourth?—husband. They'd snatched up the Woodway Resort and renovated it, jacking up the cost of the cabins, especially during hunting season and the holidays. Wanda erroneously became convinced Aurora was signaling a thieving partner at the resort across the lake from their three-thousand square foot house while her jet-set hubby "wheeled and dealed" in real estate all over the country. Aurora never forgave Wanda for the scandalous accusations. However, she eventually left town in a cloud of disgrace after becoming involved with some shady men too soon after her hubby died in a hunting accident.

"When did this happen?"

"About two weeks ago." Henry rocked back on his heels with a smirk.

"Who bought it?" Wanda had never been inside the place but had thought it would have sold by now. The view of the lake and woods made it a prime piece of real estate . . . for a price. Trouble was, few in this area had that kind of cash floating around.

"A retired attorney from Dallas. Didn't catch the name. She has a daughter in Waco and another one in Abilene so she thought this would be a great summer family place for them to gather."

"And the rest of the year?" Wanda worried about a house of that size remaining vacant.

"From what I understand she will live there but also keep her condo in downtown Dallas. Don't ask me why." He threw up his hands and closed his register.

Henry, being a small town resident all his life, abhorred the traffic and noise of the metropolis. Wanda found it exhilarating—in small doses, that is.

"In fact, the daughter in Waco's teenaged son and daughter are staying there to clean and spruce it up before the van arrives since it had been vacant for so long. Think they are both in college. So far, they have been in four times in the past two weeks buying paint, light bulbs, you name it."

"Thanks for letting me know."

He grinned. "If I hear of more, I'll give you a buzz."

Wanda made a mental note to get with the Kings—who lived down the way from the Stewart home and were neighborhood watch volunteers—to go with her to deliver a newcomer packet. Another note—finish putting the packets together tonight.

She finished visiting the other merchants she'd plan to chat with and began to meander home. The sun evaporated the cloud cover as it hovered lower in the western sky, raising the temperature into the high eighties. Darn that weatherman. How can they make a living getting things wrong so much?

Wanda stopped at a bench near the curb and set her purse down so she could dig her sunglasses out. She decided to also remove her light sweater. As she did, her gold chain necklace hooked on the top button. She sat down to unwind it before it broke. That's when it dawned on her.

Necklace. Beverly now sold expensive necklaces. *Oh, dear.*

She slumped forward and cupped her chin in her hands. Should she suggest Jimmy Bob patrol Anna's Antiques more often on Tuesday when the next puzzle came out? Or would that, as her mother used to say, only

Julie B Cosgrove

borrow trouble?

CHAPTER 20

That evening she drove into town and stopped by Good Gravy before the Friday night dinner crowd invaded.

Anne greeted her with a smile and firm handshake.

"Thanks for meeting with me, Anne. I won't keep you long. This is a survey the police department and I devised. We want to know how this community can better guarantee your safety, and that of your business." She glanced around the room at the pre-set tables with sparkling silverware and votive candles glimmering like fireflies dancing in the twilight. "Everything looks so nice. Serene. It is so hard to find a place you can actually dine and have a conversation these days."

Anne clasped her hands. "Exactly right. This is what I wanted to bring to Scrub Oak. Good food over meaningful moments."

"That would be a great bi-line in any future

advertisements."

"You know, you're right." Anne's eyes gleamed. "Thanks for the idea."

Wanda waved it away. "What is that delectable aroma?"

"Asparagus au Gratin. Lower calories but you'd never know it." She put up her finger and dashed to the kitchen. In a moment she returned with an aluminum foil container covered by a cardboard lid. "Here. Dinner. On the house. As a thank you for your advertising idea, and your desire to ensure our safety."

Wanda opened her mouth but nothing came out. What a wonderful, generous lady. She'd definitely be an asset to Scrub Oak.

Anne touched her sleeve. "I hear what people whisper. I do not blame you in the least for what happened to me or to Gloria, or that nice Irishman." She waved the survey. "And I know the other proprietors appreciate your efforts. I will fill this out tonight after closing. And you are in my prayers, Wanda."

Wanda thanked her, blinked the shimmer from her eyes, and left feeling warmer inside than her hands on the take-away container. All the way home her car smelled wonderful, making her stomach demand to be sated. "All right. Soon." Wanda pressed her midsection.

Once home, she quickly fed Sophie after letting her out to do her doggy duty. Then, she raised the lid and found the Asparagus au Gratin along with wild rice pilaf and a blackened chicken breast saturated with a ladle of creamed gravy.

She gobbled every last bite. Then she sat down and began to work on the next Hangman puzzle and Words-in-Word series since the current one would be concluding soon. Might as well think positive and assume families would want the word puzzles to continue, right? Which reminded her, she'd better also start working on that parenting article, too.

W.

On Monday, Wanda dropped off her article along with the new Hangman puzzle and Words-in-Word puzzles. "In case there is a hacker, I thought it might be better to deliver these in person."

Vicki nodded and tapped her temple. "Good thinking. I will get right on these and go over them with Mason."

Then, Wanda met up with the Kings and walked up the hill to the newly purchased Stewart house. They started along the winding sidewalk half hidden amongst shady oaks and elms. Two squirrels chatted at each other as they dashed between the branches, making a celestial highway of the twigs and budding leaves.

"Your mother showed me her new acquisitions." Wanda mentioned it because Kathy King was Beverly's daughter.

"I know." Kathy rolled her eyes. "She showed them to me, too. I'm not sure what's gotten into her. Those baubles cost a pretty penny."

Jay King sighed. "I'm working up an insurance policy rider for her now. No telling how long they will sit in that display. I mean, who around here are going to buy things like that?"

Wanda nodded toward the sprawling ranch-style at the end of the sidewalk. "Maybe the attorney who bought this place?"

He chuckled as he walked up the stoop onto the expansive covered porch, complete with ceiling fans and wicker furniture. Wanda almost expected the maid in a crisp white apron to waltz around the corner with a tray of lemonade or sweet tea.

Jay pressed the doorbell button. A melodic tune, which Wanda had heard but couldn't quite recall, sounded inside.

Kathy began to hum it.

You Are My Sunshine. That was it. What a strange choice.

No one answered.

Jay knocked on the thick wooden door painted in a deep red.

They waited. No sound of footsteps from inside.

Kathy shaded her eyes and scanned the house.

"Maybe they are still asleep?"

"At ten in the morning?" Jay scoffed.

"They are kids, dear."

He harrumphed and went around to the lakeside. Wanda and Kathy followed, traipsing through the grass that needed a good mowing and trim before the grandmother arrived. In the back stood a wheelbarrow filled with a bag of mulch and two flats of vincas.

"Guess they plan on planting those in the urns along the back patio." Kathy pointed to the covered area that almost spanned the entire length of the back of the home.

Wanda glanced around and froze.

There on the back steps coming down the porch onto an expanse of flagstone lay muddy sneakers, discarded topsy turvy. But beneath the sod-clumped cleats peeked traces of turquoise.

"Let's go. We can leave the brochure and a note on the front porch."

Her heart pounded in her chest as she scurried around to the front, stumbling a bit as she dug in her purse for a pen. She scrawled a quick hello note and placed it on the table between two wicker rockers on the porch.

"What's wrong?" Kathy stood on the steps with a concerned expression.

"Nothing. This place gives me the creeps, that's all." Wanda zipped past her.

Jay called after her. "Little wonder given your past

with the previous owner."

And possibly the present with the new one's grandkids.

Low Carb Asparagus au Gratin

Ingredients

- 10 oz fresh asparagus, trimmed and blanched in boiling water for 5 minutes.
- 2 tbs butter, melted (I used salted for this)
- ½ tsp garlic paste, or freshly minced garlic
- ½ tsp dried thyme
- Two shakes each of salt and pepper
- ½ c. shredded mozzarella cheese
- ¼ c. cream cheese, softened*

Directions

1. Preheat the oven to 400° F.
2. Arrange the asparagus in a baking dish. I alternate the stems and the flowerets every other one so when you spoon it into each serving has a floweret.
3. Melt together the butter, garlic, dried thyme, and cream cheese over medium low heat in a saucepan, stirring constantly until well blended. Pour it evenly over the asparagus.
4. Season with salt and pepper, then cook in the oven for 8-10 minutes.

5. Sprinkle the cheese over the asparagus and return the dish to the oven. Continue to cook about 4-5 minutes or until the cheese has melted and started to turn golden brown.

*Note: The Philadelphia brand whipped cream cheese is already softened and saves time.

Julie B Cosgrove

CHAPTER 21

Wanda wondered if she should inform Todd about the muddy tennis shoes. Henry at the hardware store told her the grandkids had been here a few weeks sprucing up Aurora's abandoned homestead. And they had bought paint and supplies. The robberies started soon afterward. Coincidence? She wondered.

He couldn't exactly haul someone in for wearing tennis shoes with turquoise soles, right? Even so, she knew he and the rest of Scrub Oak's finest had their eyes peeled for the tell-tale footwear on people's feet so no one would see a pair discarded on a back patio. Halfway home she made up her mind to at least let someone at the station know. She stopped to pull out her phone.

Reagan answered. "Hey Mrs. W. What's up?"

Wanda told her. She could tell Reagan wrote it down because she asked her to repeat several things.

"Okay. I'll let the guys know. In the meantime, stay safe."

Wanda responded that she would. Then she hung up. Duty done.

Seeing those shoes bothered her the rest of the morning, though. Had her message been received? Did anyone do anything about it?

She thumped her forehead. She forgot to mention the new merchandise in Anna's Antiques to Reagan. *Oh, what's with my memory lately?* She needed to read more, do more word puzzles, keep the grey cells active. *Use it or lose it.* That's what she'd heard in the Alzheimer prevention commercials.

Well, she would use it now. Wanda glanced at the clock. It read 11:47. Todd should be getting up about now. If not, he should be. She punched the second button on her phone then heard the pitchy tune as it dialed his number.

He answered on the third ring. "Hey, Aunt Wanda, What's up?"

Sounded rather chipper. She guessed he'd already had coffee. "Two things actually. Do you recall what the word will be in tomorrow's answer in the Hangman?"

His sigh came through loud and clear. "Sure. Necklace. Let me guess. You saw some lady wearing an expensive bauble."

"No, actually I saw the muddy, turquoise-soled tennis shoes of some college-aged newcomers."

"Huh?"

"But more on that in a minute. Returning to the first topic, Beverly at Anna's Antiques just got in some heirloom jewelry. Three necklaces from the early 1900s. One had a price tag of three thousand dollars."

He whistled one long, and loud, note.

She pulled her phone away and rubbed her ear, then continued to tell him about each one. And the fact Beverly had no alarm system.

"Doesn't surprise me. Several of the merchants have yet to install them. We have all encouraged them, though. This isn't 1960 anymore."

As if he knew what life was like back then. She did. She rode her bike around Scrub Oak, swung off the cypress branches into the lake, and giggled as she and Betty Sue played hide and seek through the maze with the other children at the Ferguson Mansion's annual Halloween bash. Those were the days.

Her mind returned to the present, and Todd's voice.

". . . even gave them fliers on several reputable security companies."

"Really? Beverly didn't seem to recall that. In fact, she asked me if I knew of one. I told her to contact Jay." Wanda scratched her head. "Anyway, I thought y'all might want to beef up the patrols around her shop tomorrow . . . just in case."

"I will run that by the chief. Now what is this about

muddy shoes?"

She explained that as well. "Honestly. I wasn't snooping. I simply—"

"—I know, went to greet them as part of the newcomer thing." He interrupted her with another sigh. "Look, I greatly appreciate you letting me know, I do. Much better than you organizing a stakeout of Aurora's."

How did he know that had floated through her mind?

"Try not to worry. I'll let Jimmy Bob and the chief know about these things. Now, go collect those surveys, and we will all see you tomorrow afternoon at one here at the station to go over the results."

"Right." She grimaced. She'd forgotten about picking them up from the merchants today. As soon as she hung up, her phone chimed with the reminder.

Wanda rolled her eyes. "Got it. Thanks, smart phone."

She parked in the lot behind Good Gravy and walked around downtown picking up the surveys and chatting with the owners. Many told her of their suggestions even though they had written them down. And she heard some great ones.

✓ Everyone should have the other merchants' contact numbers.

✓ The merchants should form their own watch group and meet monthly to build up camaraderie. They could also cross-promote each other if someone was having a sale or special.

✓ Beverly said those that didn't have alarms should ban together and see if they could get a discount with the same company.

✓ Anne suggested they should team up when heading to the bank with the daily deposits, a buddy system.

✓ Henry suggested they pitch in and hire a carrier to take their deposits by armored car.

Wanda gathered them up and took them home. Her tootsies throbbed from all the walking she'd done lately. She soaked her feet as she wrote up a report outlining the suggestions for the meeting Tuesday afternoon with Chief Brooks, Todd, and Jimmy Bob.

A knock sounded at her door. Evelyn. She could tell by the rhythm. At least the woman felt like leaving the house. Good sign.

She rose and opened the backdoor to find her neighbor on the stoop with a takeout bag from the Hook & Owl. "Compliments of Ray. In thanks for taking a proactive stance about these robberies and to let you know he doesn't blame you now."

She sputtered. "How is he? Headaches gone?" On Saturday he'd appeared very pale and left the fundraiser early complaining of a pounding head and slight dizziness.

"Right as rain, as they say. Enough stew for two in

here. And soda bread along with rhubarb pie."

Wanda laughed and motioned for Evelyn to step inside. "Well, you better help me eat it then." If her merchant friends kept feeding her like this, Zelda would get on her case when she weighed in on Wednesday.

The stew hit her taste buds with delight. Neither spoke for a few minutes as they shoveled in their dinner. Then Evelyn sat back and wiped her mouth. "Yummy. It is so good to taste and smell again. Thank you for the mercy run to the drug store."

"No problem."

"I'm glad people are not whispering about you anymore."

Wanda's shoulders relaxed. "Me, too. It kinda hurt my feelings. But I guess I can't blame them."

She rose to clear away their dishes then slapped her hand on the counter. "But gosh, people know me, Ev. I have helped solve several crimes and received an award from the mayor. Why would I, chairperson of the neighborhood watch, possibly . . ."

Wanda couldn't finish her sentence. Salty water clouded her vision.

Evelyn rose and laid a hand on her shoulder. "Eat some rhubarb pie. I'll make *you* a pot of tea this time. You'll feel better."

Wanda did as Evelyn suggested, not that it helped much.

That night, as she crawled under the covers, she prayed tomorrow morning would be without incident and Beverly would open her shop to nothing stolen.

Julie B Cosgrove

CHAPTER 22

Sometimes God doesn't answer our prayer the way we would like. Wanda's phone rang at eight forty-five Tuesday morning. The caller's tune from Dragnet meant only one thing. Todd hadn't gone to sleep yet. Not good news.

Her hand trembled as she reached to answer. "Hello? Todd?"

"Hey, Aunt Wanda. I hate to tell you but—"

Wanda sat upright in her bed and gasped. "—No! Oh, please don't tell me."

"Yeah. Jimmy Bob patrolled about a half hour ago. He saw a dark figure dash out the back of Anna's Antiques. He entered through the pried-opened door and found the glass cabinet at the register smashed. The jewelry gone."

Tears clogged her throat. "Is Bev all right?'

"Mad as a cat who just had a bath in the sink. But unharmed. She had not arrived yet, thank goodness. Slept in for some reason."

"God's mercy." Wanda took in a breath, realizing she'd been holding it. "Did anyone else see anything? I mean in broad daylight for goodness' sake."

"Nope. Downtown is quiet before the shops open. Except for the few workers at the courthouse and town hall. And of course, the Grocery Mart, but that is several blocks away."

Wanda had no words. A rarity, she had to admit. After a moment she swallowed and cleared her throat. "What does the chief say?"

"He wants you to come in now, Aunt Wanda. And bring the surveys."

His tone didn't sound pleasant now. Stern, professional like the one police use to read someone their rights.

"Give me a half hour to dress and grab some breakfast." Though she doubted her tightly twisted tummy would accept any.

"I'll let him know."

"Todd, you know I didn't—"

"—Aunt Wanda, I have to be objective. Concentrate only on the facts. The means, the motive, and the opportunity."

"And exactly what would my motive be? Do I own

turquoise-soled tennis shoes or look like a young athletic woman?" Her tone had escalated but she couldn't help it. Part of her wanted to throw her cell phone against the wall.

Todd didn't respond at first. Then his voice became quieter. "See you in thirty minutes. Okay?"

"Sure. Right."

She hung up and turned into her pillow for a good cry. Sophie curled up at her head, a front paw on her cheek.

W.

Neither Betty Sue nor Evelyn had phoned by the time she left. Maybe they didn't know yet. As Wanda drove into town, she felt every eye focus on her. These people knew her. The chief knew her. Surely no one suspected her involvement in these crimes after all she'd done to prove her concern for this community and its merchants?

She parked in front of the police station and slithered out of her car, half expecting paparazzi cameras to flash. But this was Scrub Oak. *Enough. Get a grip.* By golly, she'd hold her head high like any innocent woman. Wanda raised her chin, slipped her purse in the crook of her arm, and strutted into the police station like the outstanding citizen her reputation had awarded her.

"They are in the conference room." Reagan pointed to the left with her head, her expression unreadable.

Wanda nodded and walked slowly, trying not to make

her heels click. She had purposely dressed in her most conservative skirt and blouse. So why did she feel as if she wore an orange jump suit walking the green mile? She tapped on the partially opened door. It swung open as the hinges complained in a small screech.

The three men in uniform had the dignity to rise in her presence. It didn't escape her that they all sat on one side and she the other. Todd held out a chair for her, but she refused it.

She folded her arms, standing with her feet pressed to the industrial tile floor. "Is this an interrogation? Where is the tape recorder and two-way glass?"

Okay, snarky response. She had to admit her blood bubbled. How dare they?

"Mrs. Warner, um Wanda, please have a seat." Chief Brooks motioned to the pulled-out chair and then glanced up at her nephew, still standing with his hands on the back of it. "Martin, why don't you bring your chair around and sit next to her. Might ease the tension."

He seated Wanda and then did as the chief requested.

"This is simply a conference, my dear lady. Planned for later today, but under the circumstances I decided to bump it up. I appreciate you coming in early."

Fair enough. She gave him a quick smile. As if on cue, Reagan entered with cold bottles of water for everyone and took a seat as well. She nodded to Wanda with warmth in her eyes, which made Wanda relax a tad.

Having another female in the room helped even if she wore a blue uniform.

"Do you want my report on the surveys? I brought them and also a score sheet I put together last night."

Chief Brooks spread out his fingers to stop her. "In a minute. First, a few questions. We know you told Todd about the new shipment of necklaces. Mrs. Newby confirmed she showed them to you and then you two discussed the fact that she should get an alarm system." He paused.

"Yes, I did. So?" Wanda unscrewed the cap from her water and took a swig.

"Who else did you tell about this?"

He may have well taken the rest of the bottle and splashed it on her face. She sputtered. "Well, I don't think, I mean, I'm not sure. Reagan and Todd." She nodded to them. "Maybe Evelyn Jacobs my next door neighbor. We had supper together last night." She gazed into the chief's face. "Compliments of Ray O'Mallory as a thank you for my proactive stance on better security for the merchants downtown."

There she'd said it.

The police officers glanced at each other and Jimmy Bob wiggled in his seat.

"You have no explanation to why these robberies occur when *The Gazette* posts your puzzles, and that they all relate to the place or items stolen?" Chief Brooks tapped his pen on the table.

"None whatsoever. Trust me this irritates me no less than it does you. In fact, I consider it a personal insult against my being the founder and chairperson of the neighborhood watch. Not to mention that this has been my hometown since the age of nine and I don't appreciate that someone is depriving it of security and peace."

Todd cleared his throat. "Who came up with the idea of publishing these puzzles?"

She chuckled. "You, from what I'm told. Mason and Vicki said y'all discussed it over dinner about a month ago."

His face reddened. He looked at his cuticles. "Right. I recall."

"Enlighten us." The chief leaned back and tucked his thumbs in his belt.

Todd sucked in a long breath. "We talked about how to make the newspaper more family orientated. I told them how I used to . . ." He coughed in his fist. ". . . sit next to Aunt Wanda as a kid and we'd work the word puzzles together. It was our together time." He shrugged.

Wanda smiled at him and reached to pat his hand. "Special for me as well."

He slipped his hand away and recovered his policeman-like composure with a lift of his chin. "They asked if she was any good at it and I said that she was excellent. Always has been. I guess they took it from there." He glanced at her as his mouth curled up in a quick smile for half a second.

The chief grunted. "Jimmy Bob. Reagan. Do you have any ideas about this?"

The two shook their heads. From their expressions Wanda could see they felt uncomfortable about this whole meeting.

"Someone is feeding info to the perp. If it isn't one of the Clyburns or you, Mrs. Warner, then who?"

"You didn't discover any hackers?" Wanda leaned toward the chief and looked him in the eye.

He returned the gesture. "No, not that we can tell. One of the tech guys from Cleburne examined *The Gazette's* computer where Mason posts the edition. He couldn't detect any unusual activity."

Wanda thought for a moment. "Wait. Todd, can't somebody post something ahead of time and set it to publish at another time?"

"Sure."

"Then we need to find out when Mason sets it to publish digitally. My guess is at a minute after midnight. A common time to set up previously designed posts to transmit, from what I'm told. If so, that would give the thief plenty of time to plan these burglaries, don't you think?"

All the police personnel exchanged glances.

Wanda sat back with a grin on her face. "Now can we

go over the survey? I have to be at the church to help plan for May Fest."

CHAPTER 23

The rest of the meeting took about ten minutes. Chief Brooks said he would personally phone each merchant and thank them for their responses to the survey. The Sunday after May Fest, he would ask the City Council to call a meeting and invite all the downtown businesspeople to discuss putting some of these suggestions into action. He would propose it to be held in the evening since all of their establishments would be closed. Of course, the Chamber of Commerce and the mayor would be asked to attend as well.

Wanda scoffed and whispered to Todd, "They may as well invite the whole town, then."

He smirked.

With that the meeting adjourned and Wanda walked down the hall to leave. Todd caught up with her. "Thanks for coming."

"You're leaving, too?"

"Yeah. Haven't been to sleep yet."

She rubbed his bristly cheek. "I could tell."

He chuckled and held the door open for her.

"Need a ride home, Todd?"

"Nah. I am going to walk. Need to mull over a few things. Thanks, though. See ya Thursday, if not before."

She watched him saunter off, his hands thrust deep in his pockets. What had all that been about? Who knew?

She got in her car and drove the short way to the church just in time to set up for the women's luncheon followed by the May Fest committee in the fellowship hall. When she entered with the tablecloths, things became eerily quiet again. The old memory of walking in on girls talking about her in middle school reared up in her mind. But these were church folk, many of whom she'd worshiped with for decades.

She set the bundle down and raised her hands in front of her. "I know. Anna's Antiques was robbed of some new pieces of jewelry this morning and yes—spoiler alert—*necklace* is the clue to the Hangman puzzle in today's *Gazette*. I have been consulting with the police for the last hour about these strange incidences so I'd prefer not to discuss it any further."

There. Said and done. She hated that she seemed so abrupt but these burglaries stomped on her last nerve.

Pastor Bob stepped forward. "I suggest we all pray

about this and quit gossiping about it. Scripture tells us to lift each other up and not to let tongues wag."

They all shuffled around him and bowed their heads as he asked for guidance to be given to the police and investigators and to protect the community from further crime. And that the ones responsible would be brought to justice.

Wanda sniffled the emotions back. Even after Pastor's mild admonition and prayer, she sensed some of the committee members acting rather coolly toward her during the luncheon and even more so during the meeting as they finalized what needed to be done for their festivities and by whom. Did they think she'd pass the information on to thieves?

She couldn't blame them, though. Until the culprit had been caught and the mystery revealed, speculation would only become more rampant around town.

The best way to nip this in the bud, as far as she was concerned, was to find the robber and the informant—if they were two different people. Her bet lay on the newcomers, even if they were the grandkids of a wealthy Dallas attorney. Though not likely suspects, some apples can fall far from the tree, she supposed, and with the right wind, roll into rebellion. Maybe these two had.

How could she find out other than tailing them around town? Would it be wrong to send word out to the watch volunteers to help her spy on them? She pulled Pastor Bob aside to ask him.

"Depends. If you suspect them of wrongdoing it would seem right. But where do you draw the line between protecting others and violating individual rights?"

She had to agree. "Guess a pair of dirty sneakers and the fact they have been in town only a few weeks isn't enough of a reason, huh?"

He laid a hand on her shoulder, and she immediately felt his wisdom seep through to her heart. "Wanda, the last thing we want is to dissuade newcomers to our community. And, I hate to say this, my friend, but consider who their relative is. A wrongful act could go sour very quickly."

He spoke truth to her. She whispered okay and told him she'd be back later to help make paper flowers for the cakewalk booth, a new feature this year. Which reminded her. She had offered to make a Coca-Cola cake.

Wanda put a tickler in her phone to go buy the ingredients. And a new pan. Hers had years of baking stains on it, and this type of cake had to be given away in the dish it had baked in. Perhaps an aluminum one would work. Yes, definitely. Unless she saw a glass one on sale at Thrifty Treasures.

Southern Coca-Cola Chocolate Cake

Ingredients

Coca-Cola Chocolate Cake:
- 1 c. of room-temperature Coca-Cola
- ½ c. buttermilk (if you don't have buttermilk, substitute a ½ teaspoon of lemon juice, cream of tartar, or vinegar to a ½ cup of whole milk.)
- 2 tsp pure vanilla extract
- 2 c. all-purpose flour, sifted
- ¼ c. unsweetened cocoa powder
- 1 tsp baking soda
- 1 c. butter, softened
- 1 ¾ c. granulated sugar
- 2 eggs
- 1 ½ c. miniature marshmallows

Coca Cola Chocolate Icing:
- ½ cup butter, room temperature or softened
- 1/3 cup Coca Cola soda
- 3 tablespoons unsweetened cocoa powder
- 4 cups powdered sugar (confectioners' sugar)
- 2 teaspoons of pure vanilla extract

Instructions:

1. Preheat oven to 350° F. Lightly oil then dust with

flour a 13- x 9-inch baking pan.

2. In a small bowl, combine the Coca-Cola soda, buttermilk and vanilla extract. Set it aside.

3. In medium-sized bowl, sift together the flour, cocoa powder, and baking soda. Set it aside as well.

4. In large bowl, beat on low speed with a handheld mixer (Or I guess you could use a large electric wand but I still use my harvest gold electric eggbeater that was a wedding present in 1976.) the butter and sugar until combined and smooth. Add eggs, one at a time, and beat until blended.

5. Starting with the flour mixture you set aside, beat in a little at a time alternating with the Coca-Cola mixture. Continue to beat for 2 additional minutes until the batter is light and fluffy. Fold in the marshmallows with a spatula.

6. Pour the cake batter into the prepared baking dish. It is normal for the marshmallows to float to the top of the cake batter when cooking, so don't worry about that.

7. Bake approximately 15-20 minutes, then rotate the pan to ensure even cooking. Bake for another 15-20 minutes.*

8. While the cake is baking, prepare the Coca-Cola Chocolate Icing. Do not make the frosting far in advance. You need to pour it over the cake shortly

after it is through baking.

9. Remove the cake from the oven to a cooling rack. While the cake is still hot, pour the prepared Coca-Cola Chocolate Icing over cake and spread evenly to cover the entire cake to the edges.

10. Let cake cool completely before serving. Cut into squares. Serve alone or with a scoop of French vanilla ice cream. Blue Bell is a Texas favorite.

*Note: Once you reach 30 minutes, check cake every few minutes until done. Cake is done when a toothpick inserted in the center of the cake comes out clean.

This is a bit time consuming to make and requires washing a lot of bowls, but trust me. Every time I serve it, my guests roll their eyes in delight. And for potlucks, it is easy to transport since it stays in the baking dish.

Julie B Cosgrove

CHAPTER 24

Wednesday afternoon, Wanda walked into the high school gymnasium and headed to the back where Coach Lozano's office stood. He greeted her halfway on the court. "Mrs. Warner. Good to finally meet you face to face though your reputation proceeds you."

She tentatively held out her hand. "I hope it's not that bad."

He laughed. "Oh, dear woman. Not at all. My second year here you received an award from the mayor. I whistled through my teeth the loudest."

And they were the whitest she'd seen on a middle-aged man in a while. Next to the soft café colored skin and the wave of black hair that curled on his collar, if she was thirty years younger . . .

The laugh lines next to his eyes grew deeper the wider he smiled. He made her feel, well, worthy. Encouraged.

Competent. No wonder the team had soared in the standings over the past few years.

He led her into his domain. A slight odor of sweaty socks and leather hung in the air. Typical sports area. She thanked him as he offered her a chair opposite his desk. As she sat, she pushed aside the idea that hundreds of clammy legs had also sat there.

"Do you only coach the boys?"

"Mostly. Suellen coaches the girls' volleyball team, and Coach Smith is in charge of varsity football, but I am head coach over all the high school teams. And I supervise the gym classes for both girls and boys, too. Why do you ask?"

"You've heard about the robberies in the past few weeks, yes?'

He rocked back in his chair. "I have. But why come to me?"

"According to two witnesses, the culprit wore athletic shoes with turquoise soles. Both believed the person to be a young, tall female."

"Ah. I see. And you want to know if that rings any bells."

"Exactly."

He leaned forward and interlaced his arms together. "The police already questioned me. I told them I knew of no student who wore those shoes. To do so would be disloyal."

"Right. But here is my other question. How common would it be for a young woman, say under twenty-five and fit, to lift and swing a twenty-five pound bag?"

"Most athletic women can easily lift up to 90 pounds in stationary weights. But a bag is a bit different. It moves and is larger. Let me see."

He put on a pair of readers and peered at his computer screen, keying in something, and scrolling through with his mouse. "This article says the average untrained in weightlifting female under thirty should easily lift fifty pounds of dead weight. But I've seen teenage girls grunt and struggle to pass a thirty-five pound medicine ball in gym class. Why did you want to know?"

"Gloria Longoria, who owns the Bird Nest, was whacked semi-conscious with a twenty-five pound sack of birdseed."

"Aw." He stood. "Which means a person would have to grab it from the shelf, swing it around and up and wham." He mimed it, his hands landing inches from Wanda's head.

She flinched.

"Sorry." He sat back down. "You have to consider the adrenaline that could have been flowing at the time. Even so, I agree if the assailant was a female, she would have to be fairly fit to accomplish such a thing."

"And no one comes to mind?"

He shook his head slowly, eyes focused in space as if

he went down a list of names in his mind. "I have an idea. We could hold a new contest for May Fest. Who can throw a medicine ball over their head the furthest wins two free tickets to the baseball playoffs in Elgin the first weekend in June, heh? Our team is one win away from qualifying."

"Yes, I've heard." The prospect of Scrub Oak heading for the finals had been the buzz of the town for weeks, which was why she'd made it the fifth clue in the Hang Man puzzle. That fact didn't escape her, especially since it came out in two days on Friday morning.

He raised his eyebrows. "What do you think, then?"

"Okay. It's not a bad idea." *Though I doubt the thief would participate.* "Let me run it by our church committee and I'll get back with you."

They shook hands and he rose to open the door for her.

She left somewhat relieved. What did Coach have that someone would want to steal? Sports equipment? The idea seemed ludicrous—and that might be a good thing, come to think of it. Come Friday, everyone would solve the Hangman clue and no reports of a burglary would come into the police station. Then townsfolk would know the robberies had been only a coincidence. They had nothing to do with her word puzzles.

A pressing weight evaporated from her shoulders. Wanda walked back through the gymnasium with a lighter step than when she'd entered.

Then she stopped. Had she heard hurried footsteps shuffling away in the opposite direction? She turned slowly in place as she scanned the gym. No one walked amongst the bleachers or along the edges of the highly polished floor to the locker rooms. Through the frosted half glass of the coach's office door, she noticed his shadow. He hadn't left.

Weird. Had someone been listening to their conversation then scurried away when she came out of the office? Wanda shook off the premonition and pushed through the double doors into the ninety-degree heat.

Julie B Cosgrove

Thursday morning, Wanda grabbed the folder with the next Hangman and Words-in-Word puzzles and took them to *The Gazette*. She entered the newspaper office and smiled at Vicki.

"My, you're chipper this morning." Vicki leaned back in her chair.

"Tomorrow the spy glass will no longer be on us." Wanda tapped the desk.

"How do you figure? I feel like it is too focused on us. We keep getting notes slipped under the door, comments on the website, and a few in-person rants about how this rash of robberies are due to the word puzzles."

"Partially my fault, I admit." Mason leaned against the entry into the reception area. "My hand still stings from the mayor's slap." He shook it vigorously and winked.

Wanda snickered. "Well, tomorrow's answer is *Elgin,*

about the baseball team heading to the finals." She crossed her fingers. "Unless someone steals third base, we are safe."

The couple groaned at her pun. Vicki eased her swollen body from the desk and waddled to her husband's side. "You may be right, though. I mean what does Coach Lozano have that a robber would want?"

Mason rubbed his hand across her lower back. "Sure, you want to keep coming in? I mean, we are getting close to D-Day and you seem really uncomfortable."

"I'm fine. I would go nuts at home." She pecked his cheek.

Wanda smiled. Such a sweet couple. She hated to intrude, but she had to get on with her day. "I came to drop off the next Hangman puzzle and corresponding Words-in-Word puzzles in hopes you decide to continue them despite recent events. I figure the rest of this week will get fairly hectic with May Fest starting up on Sunday. Seems earlier and earlier each year."

Mason huffed a long breath out of his cheeks. "Thank you. Yes, we do plan on it, and having them this soon will help out."

"Oh, and Vicki. I'll email you the corrected article on parenting later today after I finish helping to make the decorations for my church's May Fest booth. Thanks for your suggestions on how to make it better."

Vicki smiled. "You've done really well for a rookie. I

look forward to reading it."

"Is there anything else I can do for y'all?" Wanda passed her gaze between the two of them.

Mason stepped closer and whispered into her ear. "Catch the burglar."

"That's Todd's job, not mine. He keeps making that point very clear." She let off a nervous laugh and set her folder on Vicki's desk. "Bye, now."

All the way home Mason's plea echoed in her ears. More and more the two young adults at Aurora's old house seemed the likely candidates. She ticked off the reasons.

- ✓ New in town so few would recognize them.
- ✓ Young so probably more fit.
- ✓ Muddy tennis shoes.
- ✓ Arrival just before the burglaries began.

The last one stuck on her tonsils. Did the fact they renovated her nemesis' previous homestead color her opinion? Or, could somehow Aurora be getting back at Wanda for being the catalyst to drive her out of town? Well, the woman had done that on her own, but she probably blamed Wanda rather than admit to her own mistakes.

No. Wanda shook it from her thoughts. That made no sense. Aurora had no control over who purchased her old home, right? Even if she had lived in Dallas for twenty some odd years and married husbands two and three there, it didn't mean she and this retiring attorney traveled in the same circles. On the other hand, money drew Aurora like the melody of an ice cream truck draws kids, and this attorney obviously had a bundle of cash. There must be a way Wanda could find out the attorney's name without attracting suspicion.

Ah, hah. Of course. Bake cookies and bang on the door. Introduce herself. Make sure they got the newcomer packet. Chat the two kids up. They had not been home before, but maybe tomorrow they would be.

With a firm plan in place, she felt more in control than she had since these ridiculous assaults began. Loyalty to Scrub Oak, which had been simmering inside of her, bubbled to a soft boil. How dare someone mess with their serenity and security right under her nose. It made the neighborhood watch program seem inept and the police resemble the Keystone Cops. Those facts made things personal.

Time to take matters into her own hands, for the betterment of everyone. This needed to be resolved before May Fest began. The merchants and the town's economy depended upon it.

A verse from the Proverbs whispered into her thoughts. *Pride goes before destruction, a haughty spirit before a fall.*[1]

---

[1] Proverbs 16:18

She pulled into the parking lot of her church and stared at the shadow of the steeple cross splayed across the grass, pointing to her. Why did that materialize? Did the Holy Spirit try to tell her something?

Did pride taint her? Not that she wanted to be the town hero again but, in all honesty, her standing in the community meant a great deal and the fact it had been tarnished ate away at her psyche. But that was simply due to the fact she loved living in Scrub Oak. It was a very special place. Pride in one's community wouldn't be considered a sin. Would it?

Insecurity pressed against her as she entered the fellowship hall to see how the decoration making had been going. She remained quiet during most of the hands-on meeting as the group made more paper streamers, flowers, and booth signs, and then assembled sacks filled with goodies as prizes for the game winners. When they broke for coffee and snacks, Betty Sue cornered her.

"You feeling all right today? You don't seem yourself."

Wanda explained about the proverb. "Am I being prideful? I must admit, when I notice people whispering and glaring at me, it makes my skin crawl. And these burglaries seem to be a personal attack on me as well as the merchants. Is my perspective off kilter?"

Betty Sue drug her by the elbow to sit on the stage steps away from the chatter of the other volunteers. "I think there are different motives behind pride. Pride, like anger, is not in itself a sin. It's an emotion. The actions you take as a result determine that. If your pride is wholesome and good, then how can evil come from it? But if selfishness fuels pride, then that can lead to us being humbled by the Holy Spirit. God can tumble the emotional towers we build just as He did at Babel."

Wanda blinked. Betty Sue's profoundness moved her. With a shaky lower lip, she grinned and thanked her. "You are truly the best friend a gal could have."

The compliment made Betty Sue blush. "You've helped me and given me plenty of advice over the years. What are friends for?" She rose to get herself some iced tea.

Warmth coated Wanda's inside like the pink liquid in those stomach commercials. The rest of the afternoon went swiftly. At six, Wanda dragged her tired and aching muscles home for a hot bath.

Tomorrow would be another day—a good one. *The Gazette* would come out and nothing else would happen. She planned to relish in the reprieve.

CHAPTER 26

Bright and early on Friday morning, someone pounded on her backdoor. Wanda yawned. Again? What now? She padded to the kitchen as Todd peered in her backdoor, his face red. Uh, oh.

After sucking in a breath, she plastered on a smile and unlocked it. "Good morning, nephew."

He pushed through with a growl. Sophie scurried to the safety of her doggie bed. Wanda felt like following her.

She opened her mouth to ask why the foul mood so early in the morning then caught the date on her fridge calendar. Oh, no.

His fist slammed on the table. "Somebody broke into the school gymnasium just before dawn. Evidently Coach Lozano kept the fundraising money for their trip to Elgin in the bottom drawer of his filing cabinet. Over twelve-hundred dollars—gone."

She gasped and backed to sit in the kitchen chair before her knees buckled.

Todd leaned in. "He tells me you went to his office earlier this week."

"I did. To ask him if a female could easily lift large bag of bird seed over her head and sling it with enough force as to cause injury."

The vein on Todd's forehead turned blue, then purple. He sank into the chair opposite her as a guttural growl slipped through his lips.

"Aunt Wanda, why can't you stay out of police business?"

She pressed her lips in a tight line to keep the sobs from inching up her throat.

He rolled his eyes to the ceiling and then returned them to her face. "Today's answer to the Hangman puzzle is *Elgin* And the Words-in-Word happens to be *fundraiser*. Coincidence?"

"No, guess not." She picked at a cuticle. "I mean that the puzzles relate to each other, not the crime. I have no control over that."

"That's not what folks are saying. Several believe you are orchestrating this whole thing so you can be the hero again."

"What?!" Her brain could not make sense of such a thing any more than it could interpret the Book of Genesis in Mandarin or Swahili.

Todd rubbed his temples. "Two city council members phoned the chief *at home*. Woke him up and asked why you are not behind bars. Blamed it on favoritism because I'm on the force."

She sniffled. "Is your job in jeopardy?"

His facial muscles eased a tad bit. "Not yet."

Anger began to replace her confusion. She rose and paced the room. "How could they? This is ludicrous."

"Aunt Wanda. I need you to come back to the station. The town needs to see me escort you inside."

She halted as her lower jaw dropped. "Now? In my robe?"

"Well, I will allow you to get dressed. I'll feed Sophie."

Wanda blinked. How could this be happening? "In handcuffs?"

His lips slanted to one side. "I think we can skip that, but you are riding in back of the cruiser."

Her leg muscles felt like a popsicle left on the sidewalk in summer. She grasped the back of the chair to steady herself. Slowly what her nephew said sunk into her grey cells. "Very well. Give me ten minutes. I promise I won't escape out the bathroom window."

He chuckled. "You wouldn't fit."

She almost threw the chair at him. Maybe handling a bag of bird seed or a trash can lid could be feasible for a female in her sixties after all. Wanda kept that thought to herself as she turned to walk down the hall.

Todd's voice sounded behind her from the kitchen as the tinkle of kibbles hit the dog bowl. "Do you want any breakfast, Aunt Wanda?"

She called back. "Wouldn't stay down. Thanks, though."

She let the tears flow as she showered. To think two years ago they heralded her in town square. Gave her gifts and a medal. Then applauded her when she helped discover who'd conked Tom and later who graffitied the downtown area. Now, the people who had known her most of her life accused her of conniving crimes for self-glory. Of all things.

She turned the spigot to cold and splashed her face in the spray to reduce the puffiness from crying. Then she toweled, brushed her teeth, and dressed. What does one wear when being arrested?

She swished the hangers back and forth before deciding on a cream pull-over blouse with black, wrinkle-free slacks and black flat sandals. Demure, yet comfortable. Who knows how long they'd hold her? She grabbed her black lightweight cardigan in case the jail cells got cold at night or they didn't have a blanket for her.

Her feet felt encased in concrete as she shuffled back to the kitchen. With a deep sigh she nodded. "Ready. Let's go."

Todd turned her toward the doorway that led into the foyer. "Through the front door, I'm afraid. This is official."

As they walked to his police cruiser parked at the curb, with its lights swirling, Wanda imagined all of her neighbors peering through curtains. Evelyn sprinted across her lawn.

"What is going on? Todd? Wanda?"

Wanda refused to peer into her neighbor's eyes for fear of losing it right there on the sidewalk. *Please, Lord grant me dignity.* "Call Betty Sue. Pray for me."

Todd opened the back car door and pressed her head to guide her inside the vehicle.

She complied without a word.

"Sorry." His word came out in a husky whisper. She realized what this must mean to him as well. Arresting his own kin. Poor guy was just doing as he'd been ordered.

"Me, too. It's okay. Do what you must."

They drove to the police station in silence. Wanda sat back on the hard-as-steel seat. Arrestees obviously were not allowed any comforts.

At least no paparazzi dashed after them and flashed camera bulbs along the way, though several people stopped to stare while walking dogs or working in their lawns. She resisted sarcastically giving their open-mouthed faces the Queen of England's wave.

Julie B Cosgrove

CHAPTER 27

Wanda entered the Scrub Oak police station with a forced smile. Reagan scrunched her eyebrows, mouthing the word, "Sorry."

Todd led Wanda down the hall to the same conference room as before, where both Jimmy Bob and Chief Brooks sat before a spread of coffee and donuts. At first, she wanted to say something snarky like "Well, we meet again" but she decided against it. Compliance had to ooze from her pores for her sake—and Todd's.

She nodded to each of them and sat when Todd pulled out a chair for her. With hands folded across the table, she waited for one of them to speak.

Chief Brooks inspected her face. "Good morning, Mrs. Warner. Officer Todd Martin has informed you of the latest incident, I gather?"

Two days ago, she was Wanda. Why so formal now?

Then she heard the soft whir of the tape recorder. Right. Protocol. "Yes, he has."

Somewhere she recalled that a person would be wise to answer simply *yes* and *no* as much as possible and not embellish their answers. Probably from that crime show on TV that Evelyn loved to watch. Sounded like good advice at the moment as she faced the chief's stone-faced expression.

"And you are the one who designed the word puzzles to appear in today's edition of *The Gazette?*"

"Yes, I am. Though Mason has the final say when it comes to the order in which they appear." Okay, she'd answered more than *yes* or *no* but she wanted to spark their memory of the last discussion when they talked about shuffling things around. She hoped her response didn't implicate the Clyburns, though.

"Coach Lozano stated you visited his office Wednesday."

Here we go. She avoided the urge to glance at Todd who stood off to the side. "That is correct."

"The reason for the visit?"

She almost blurted out none-of-your-beeswax, but of course, that would not be totally true—or respectful.

Truth shall set you free, that's what the Bible says. *Here goes nothing.* She told them honestly knowing a reprimand would be the chief's likely response.

"I see. No other reason?"

That surprised her. She sputtered her negative answer.

"He tells us you kept studying his office."

Had she? "I'd never been in a coach's office before. I guess I felt a bit nervous. I agree my reasons for asking him the things I did might not be exactly kosher. Guess my nervousness showed."

"Did you at any time discuss the playoffs coming up?"

"Yes. It is the topic of conversation all over town. He is proud as punch of that team. It's no wonder he brought it up."

"He did, not you?'

"That is correct."

"And did he tell you of the fundraisers to help pay for this excursion?"

"The topic never came up."

"But you knew about it?"

"Yes. They have had carwashes at the school parking lot every Saturday for weeks. And bake sales on the sidewalk in front of the Grocery Mart."

Chief Brooks sighed through his nose and sat back.

Wanda turned to Todd. "Should I have an attorney present?"

Todd's tanned face paled.

Chief Brooks answered. "You are not under arrest, Mrs. Warner. Not yet, though you are a person of interest. Do you have any doctor appointments in Burleson or Fort

Worth?"

"Um, no. Not anytime soon."

"Good, then I strongly suggest you do not leave the area until our investigation has cleared you of all suspicious activities." The chief narrowed his gaze on her face. "In fact, I'd think it best if you stayed in your house right now."

She opened her mouth, then shut it again. Taking in a shaky breath, she scooted forward in the chair. "But I am a volunteer at May Fest. And it starts up on Sunday. I can't go?"

The chief glanced at Todd. He cleared his throat. "Aunt Wanda, considering the sentiment of the town right now, I don't think it is great idea. Coach Lozano is pretty high on everyone's approval list. He is not being silent in his opinion of you."

Wanda couldn't hold the tears back anymore. She pulled her hands to her face.

The chief sighed. "Interview suspended at nine-o'five." The tape recorder stopped whirring.

Without gazing up, she sniffled a thank you. She heard a chair screech and footfall leaving. In a minute Jimmy Bob set a box of tissues and a cup of water from the cooler in front of her.

"Thanks, Jimmy Bob." It came out in a squeak. She dabbed her eyes, then took a sip. "I'm sorry for that display of emotion."

The chief huffed and rubbed the back of his neck, his body language revealing he felt uncomfortable in front of a blubbering female. Honestly, who didn't? But he had the decency to wait patiently for her to calm down again.

"Are you all right now? Can we get back to the questions?'

She took a gulp of water and nodded. "Thank you."

He clicked on the tape recorder again and acknowledged the interview as continuing at nine-twelve.

"So, it is Mason Clyburn who determines when each clue is published. You have no control or influence over that?"

"Well, not necessarily." She twisted to the side to where her nephew leaned against the wall again. "If you recall, Todd, you suggested that I ask him to mix up the clues in case someone had somehow gotten the answers and had preplanned out the crimes. But yes, as the editor in chief now, he has the final say."

Chief Brook's left eyebrow arched. "Martin?"

Todd took a seat. "Obviously it didn't matter. The last two crimes happened anyway."

The chief groaned. "Mrs. Warner. People are talking. They say you are doing this to be in the limelight again. I believe you are more intelligent than that. You have done a lot for this community in the last couple of years, and I for one commend you for it."

Her face, where the tears had washed away her

foundation, turned warm. She brushed the sensation away.

"However, you are our number one suspect at the moment. You have means, and opportunity, maybe even motive."

"I may not be the only one." Wanda viewed her nephew for a second and saw his chin slightly move forward then back again. She considered it his approval to proceed.

She informed the chief of her idea of visiting newcomers and letting them know about the neighborhood watch captain assigned to them, and how she had noticed the muddy, turquoise-soled sneakers at Aurora's old house. Then how the timeline fit, and what Coach Lozano had told her about the strength of young, possibly fit females.

The chief listened, fingers tented. "Interesting, indeed. Jimmy Bob, go check it out."

"Yes, sir." The senior policeman scurried out as if glad to have a reprieve. Wanda didn't blame him in the least.

"Okay, Martin. Take your aunt home, this time without using the lights. And she can sit in the front passenger seat."

"Yes, sir."

"Mrs. Warner, you are free to move about the town if you wish. Personally, if I were you I wouldn't. Be aware this force will have you under surveillance, though."

The chief announced the time the interview had ended then turned off the recorder.

Todd pulled out Wanda's chair for her to stand and the two left the station in silence.

Julie B Cosgrove

CHAPTER 23

Wanda called her friend, DiAne Gates, who had moved away decades ago when her late husband got a job in Longview. The two had kept in touch though. Three times a year they met at the mall in Arlington for lunch, shopping, and to catch up on each other's lives.

Perhaps DiAne could come spend a few days. Her husband had passed last fall and, being a widow herself, Wanda wanted to help her friend through this tough first year. Besides, with the town turning against her, Wanda could use an *outside* friend right now.

Sure, she had Evelyn and Betty Sue, but they were busy with their own May Fest duties and to exclude them from that would be selfish. Besides, she didn't want their reputations tarnished by association. People probably recalled their involvement in the other crime solving she'd participated in over the past two years. No, it seemed best to not involve them in any way, shape, or form in this mess.

Of course, she could entertain herself for the weekend with a good novel or puttering around in her garden, but it would be nice to have someone around besides her dachshund. As she recalled, DiAne loved to play Scrabble. They both adored the British actor, the late Rex Harrison, God rest his soul. Maybe she could find some of his movies to stream on her TV.

"How fun!" DiAne's voice sounded chipper through the phone. "How did you know these four walls were starting to close in? I have a doctor's appointment this afternoon in Dallas but I can head out in the morning after my Thai-chi class and stay through lunch on Monday. Be there by noon."

Wanda hung up and held her cell phone to her chest. Then she thought of all she needed to do. Deep clean for one. Make up the guest bed and refresh the spare towels with a tumble in the dryer so they smelled nice and were dust free.

As she got out her cleaning bucket, the Holy Spirit tickled her subconscious. She should have been more honest about her modus operandi. Surely her old friend would not turn against her. But if they got stares and whispers while they were out and about in town, DiAne needed an answer as to why. Wanda called her back and fessed up.

"Oh, my. You poor soul. How dreadful for you. Your heart must be cracking in two."

Wanda felt the tears rising in the back of her throat again. Nope, no more. She took a gulp of iced tea. "I wanted you to know what's going on. And I would understand if you decided not to come."

"Pfft. They don't tar and feather anymore in your town, do they?"

Wanda laughed. She loved this gal. "Not that I know of, though a few folks do raise chickens."

"We'll avoid them, then. See you soon."

"Great. Looking forward to it. I'll have lunch ready." Wanda's burdened spirit lightened like an empty suitcase.

"Wonderful. And until then, you are in my prayers."

"Thanks, DiAne. Safe travels."

When she hung up, Wanda felt much better about the whole thing . . . until she heard a tap on her backdoor and saw Betty Sue's forlorn expression.

When she opened the door, her friend swished in on a cloud of lavender and vanilla. "Oh, you poor thing. I cannot believe Todd whisked you away in that police car like a common criminal. I have a few words for that boy."

Wanda pumped her hands. "It's okay. He just did his job. I am not wearing a monitor on my ankle . . . yet." She hesitated. "Are you sure you want to come in? People may be watching."

"Phooey." She swatted the idea away as she stepped

over the stoop.

The two sat at her kitchen table and discussed the whole thing.

"I am glad DiAne is coming to visit you. I have heard so much about her through the years I feel as if I already know her. But Evelyn and I would have come and sat around with you, you know that."

"You both are busy with May Fest preparations and I wouldn't think of pulling y'all away from that. Besides, like it or not you both have reputations to protect."

Betty Sue laced her arms. "Well, I'd be more than happy to boycott the whole thing just to show this town we are behind you. The nerve of some people. Honestly."

Her life-long friend's loyalty made Wanda feel all gooey inside. She reached over and side hugged her shoulders. "You are the best. Wanna make low-cal mug brownies? I have some low carb vanilla ice cream sweetened with Stevia to put on top."

"Now you're talking." Betty Sue's eyes gleamed. "You are really getting into these healthy recipes, aren't you?"

"Thanks to you. And most of them are scrumptious. Who knew?"

"Your friend hasn't seen you since you dropped thirty pounds, has she?"

"No, it's been almost a year since we met up. Her hubby passed last fall. She needed time."

Also a widow, Betty Sue understood. "Well, she is going to be pleasantly surprised, then."

They whipped together the recipe and watched the mugs spinning in the microwave, then sat down and relished the dessert as they licked their spoons without guilt.

Wanda sighed inwardly. If only life's problems could always be solved by chocolate.

Betty Sue's visit gave her courage, and she decided that, despite the police's advice, she couldn't live as a hermit. Decision made, she headed to the Grocery Mart, then changed her mind when she pulled in and three people glared at her.

Enough of that. The chief said to stay in the area. Surely that meant this county. She headed for the mega market on the highway instead. Arrest her if they wanted, she planned to have fun. Take her time, roam the aisles, and see what different things they carried that her local one didn't. And try not to feel as if she had become a turncoat for not giving her local grocery store her business.

An hour and a half later, she stuffed the sacks in her trunk, chiding herself over the amount of money she had spent on see-buy items. She had to admit, though, she did enjoy the anonymity. She drove home as the late Friday afternoon commuter traffic tied up the highway. Not even that dampened her mood. She turned on the local Christian radio station as she crept along, the same one they always played in A Cut Above. Which reminded her . . .

Wanda had to make a hair appointment. Her locks had become almost unmanageable and her style grown out enough to lose its shape. Though Carol vacationed with the Jacobs, she knew the other stylists in A Cut Above. Either would be fine with her. She prayed they were still open. She asked her phone to dial the number and thank goodness Rebecca answered.

"Well, I do have a nine o-clock cancelation in the morning with Brittanee. Would that work?"

"Perfect. See you then."

That way she could zip by Sally's when she opened at ten and buy some to-go salads and keto-friendly muffins for lunch when DiAne arrived. After the two hour drive, she'd probably want to kick back and relax. She might want to go out for dinner tomorrow night, though.

After Wanda packed away the groceries, she heard a tap on her backdoor. Evelyn waved through the glass and held up a sack.

Wanda opened the door and the whiff of french fries and cheeseburgers tantalized her nose.

Evelyn grinned. "After this morning I thought you might need carbs and a friendly face. I saw you pull in a bit ago."

Though she wanted to protect them from gossip, Wanda thanked God for her two best friends who had come to her aid after her harrowing morning. "Bless you.

Come on in. After shopping for groceries all afternoon at that mega mart on the highway, I am a tad famished. Please, sit."

"Why'd you go there?"

Wanda shrugged as she dug out the burgers and fries and put them on plates. "Too many eyes and whispers in town right now."

"Right." Evelyn cocked her head and gave her a sympathetic smile.

As they chomped on the takeout food from Better Burgers, the local hang-out, Wanda filled Evelyn in. "I had hoped Todd or Jimmy Bob would have let me know about the conversation with that lawyer's grandkids. But since they haven't, I can only surmise one of three things."

"Oh? And those are?"

Wanda counted them off on her fingers. "The kids weren't there again, it is a dead end, or they are both under strict orders from the chief not to tell me anything."

Evelyn nodded. "My guess is number three. To think Aurora might be behind this is a bit of a stretch, even for you." Evelyn pointed a crispy french fry dipped in catsup at Wanda. "Do you even know where she is?"

Wanda scoffed. "Not here."

"You sure?" Her eyes narrowed. "She might be a free woman by now if she had a good attorney. Maybe the one who bought her house."

The thought yanked away Wanda's appetite. "Then

why sell the place?"

Evelyn stirred her stew. "Would you want to come back? She sorta burned all the bridges. Of course, nowadays she could have orchestrated everything via computer chats from anywhere in the world."

"Why? To deface me?"

"Well, for one. Yes. You did humiliate her."

Wanda shook her head. "She did that all by herself." She stared at a spot on her kitchen wall to make sure it didn't move. DiAne cringed at the sight of spiders.

It did move. It left the wall and flew. Darn horse flies. She went to retrieve the swatter from the utility room. As soon as she sat back down with weapon in hand the smart bug disappeared.

"They know what that is." Evelyn pointed again, this time at the swatter.

"Seems that way." She set the thing down. "Who else could be behind all of this, Ev?"

"No clue whatsoever. But what irks me is how some folk in this town are blaming you. I have permanent teeth marks in my tongue in restraint from giving them a piece of my mind."

Wanda grinned and thanked the Lord she had at least two loyal friends, and one on the way the next day.

After Evelyn left, Wanda continued to ponder who might be behind these robberies as she tidied up and made the Coca-Cola Chocolate Cake. It did seem like a personal assault. But if not Aurora, then who else held harsh feelings against her?

Wait a minute. Maybe not to her though.

Had Mason or Vicki ticked anyone off?

Or Tom Jacobs?

Almost two years ago, someone definitely had it in for them. Could that person have somehow raised an ugly head again? As far as Wanda knew, the police never found the culprit who whacked Tom and trashed the newspaper office, though with Wanda's help they knew whodunnit. The perp had gone into the wind—wasn't that the term the TV detective used for disappearing without a trace?

The new perspective changed things quite a bit. She had not truly considered that angle before. She had been too consumed with her own pity party and wondering who had it in for her.

But she put it all aside for now. Too much to do. Maybe she would bounce this new angle off DiAne when she came.

She made up DiAne's bed then set out tiny soaps next to the sink. She'd wait until she had bathed in the morning to scrub the bathroom. Next, she did a search for Rex Harrison movies. To her surprise, he'd starred in over forty of them. Perhaps they'd choose one neither had ever seen even though she knew they'd want to see the one in which he played the pope to Michelangelo for the umpteenth time.

Excited to see her friend, Wanda settled in for the night in a much better mood than when the day had started.

Keto Mug Brownies

Ingredients:

- 1 Tbsp of melted butter
- 1 Tbsp of coconut flour or 2 tablespoons of almond flour
- 1 Tbsp of unsweetened cocoa powder
- ½ tsp of baking powder
- 1 egg, beaten until creamy
- ¼ tsp vanilla
- 1 Tbsp Lucy's sugar free mini chocolate chips
- 1 tsp finely chopped nuts if desired.*

Directions:

1. In a large coffee mug, melt the butter in the microwave for 10 seconds on high.
2. Remove to cool slightly then add the rest of the ingredients. Mix well with a fork.
3. Microwave on high for one minute—if you have

one with 900 watts or higher, check it after 50 seconds. You don't want it to become too dry. Low wattages may take 10-15 seconds longer.

4. Let it cool for two-three minutes (it'll be worth the wait —you don't want to burn your tongue!) then dig in with a spoon!

*Note: I use pecans because we love them here in Texas. And yes, it is pronounced pa-**kon** around here not pee-can.

Adding low carb, low sugar ice cream makes it even yummier. Around here, our local creamery, Braums, makes several sugar free flavors.

Julie B Cosgrove

CHAPTER 29

After a light breakfast Saturday morning, Wanda read her daily devotional, dressed, and drove to get her hair cut.

Rebecca welcomed her with lowered eyelashes. Wanda wondered why, though she dared not ask. Perhaps things progressed between her and Todd to the point of her being slightly embarrassed if Wanda knew what they did behind closed doors. She'd learned long ago not to ask about those sorts of things. She'd been raised with the rhyme that first comes love then comes marriage, then comes . . . well, people had different ideas about the order these days.

The girl barely glanced at her as Wanda paid for the trim, but when her eyes rose to give her the receipt, they conveyed something strange. Disdain? Why?

Maybe she and Todd had a fight and she thought Wanda wanted the scoop? More likely Rebecca had heard the rumors and wondered if A Cut Above would be the next target since she had been left in charge. Wanda almost told her she had not come to case the joint but decided against it. Instead, she slapped on her best little old lady smile, and left.

Not yet ten in the morning, she decided to go home and spruce the bathroom before heading to Sally's. Rebecca's reaction still got to her as she bent over the tub to scrub it down. Should she ask Todd why the girl had been so moody? That might not fare well.

Then she heard Todd's voice. Her heart skipped. Had she imagined it?

"Aunt Wanda? Are you here?"

What now? Another fake arrest? She wiped her forehead with her arm, struggled to her feet, and went down the hallway to the kitchen. "I'm here. What is it?"

He poured himself a cup of coffee. "I am here to help in the yard, remember?"

She felt the blood leave her face. "Oh, of course." Actually, she'd forgotten they'd set this date over a week ago.

"You okay?"

She wiped her hands on the dish towel. "Frankly I thought you were here to drag me back to jail." Her response carried a snarky tone. She couldn't help it. It still irritated the stuffing out of her.

He scuffed the floor with the tip of his boot. "I'm

sorry about yesterday, but orders are orders."

She sank into one of the dinette chairs. "I know. But did you have to make it so public?"

His face reddened as he handed her a freshly poured mug of java, doctored the way she liked. "I brought kolaches."

She felt her hips stretch an inch on each side at the mention of the sweet treats, especially after her burger indulgence yesterday evening with Evelyn. And the fact that in another hour or so she'd be eating lunch with DiAne.

Oh drat. She still had to get that from Sally's. Oh, well. Mending fences with Todd topped her to-do list. She thanked him and took a peach-filled pastry, relishing each bite as her nephew went to get the tools from the garage. A few minutes later she heard the lawn mower rev. What a serendipity that they had planned this before she knew DiAne would be coming.

She brought him a glass of iced water as he raked the freshly mown grass. Todd took several gulps then spoke up. "Jimmy Bob spoke to those kids. Yes, their mother knows Aurora. Evidently back in the day they were sorority sisters at SMU. But he didn't get any sense that Aurora would be involved."

"I see." She tried to sound convinced.

"The merchants are pretty antsy."

"Because of May Fest?"

"Noooo." He drew the answer out and then stopped as if wanting Wanda to think of another reason. After a moment he peered into her face. "Because the last day of the Hangman clues comes out on Tuesday. Some are talking of hiring security guards."

"Ahhh." She nodded.

"Aunt Wanda? Are you sure you're all right?" His eyes showed deep concern. "First you forget we are fixing up your yard then you—"

She swished his thought away with a wave of her hand. "I'm fine. DiAne is coming for a visit today so I have been cleaning like that white tornado commercial. Remember it?"

She could tell by his face he didn't. He set his glass down on the stoop. "I thought I smelled bleach. That's nice though. It's been a while since you got together. How is she?"

"Sounds fine over the phone, but I will find out when she gets here. We widows tend to put on a brave face."

"You still miss him?"

"Of course, it just hurts less now. The pain is more sweet than bitter."

As they continued to work in the yard, they found four gnawed stew bones, some other presents Sophie had left that Wanda had not seen to scoop, and an earring she had lost last winter.

"I thought I'd never see this again." She held it up to

her lobe. "One of my favorites. Thanks." She tucked it into her pocket with a sigh. "Wish finding the perp who's been messing with our town would be so easy to uncover."

Todd didn't respond. He took the rakes and hung them up in the garage. Then he opened the backdoor for her. "Have fun this weekend with DiAne. Stay out of trouble, okay?" Todd put on his Stetson and kissed her cheek goodbye.

Fences mended between them. Wanda's heart lightened as she headed to Sally's to pick up their lunch. If she arrived early enough, she might be the only one in the place. She could only hope.

No such luck. She'd never seen so many folks at eleven in the morning. The din of conversations diminished when she entered. Her chin set, Wanda walked up to Sally and bought two salads, muffins, and two cups of soups to go.

"Sorry, Wanda. Some people are just plain insensitive." Sally whispered it under her breath as she rang up the sale.

"Getting used to it." Wanda inserted her debit card and punched in her PIN. Then when it dinged, she yanked it out with a sigh. "Sorta."

Sally patted her arm as she handed her the take-away cartons. The sympathy in her eyes spoke volumes. At least Wanda had one merchant on her side.

Back in her car, she vowed not to let the townsfolks'

attitudes get her down. She would be proved innocent, the culprit would surface and be convicted, and she exonerated. Maybe then, people would learn a lesson in trusting their fellow citizens. The Constitution claimed everyone to be innocent until proven guilty for heaven's sake.

She'd barely gotten home and put her things in the fridge when she heard a horn toot. She dashed to the front as DiAne emerged from her tan sedan, waving.

The two squealed in unison and hugged, bouncing a bit on the balls of their feet. Wanda observed a few front curtains flutter across the street. No matter. She hugged her friend again. "Well, welcome to Scrub Oak."

"My, you look great. How much weight have you lost? If it's something in the water here I may be staying for a while."

She laughed. "Come on inside. The heat is enough to wilt you."

Wanda helped DiAne carry her luggage to the guest room and then left her to freshen up as she set out their meal.

DiAne emerged and smiled at the cardboard bowls and styrene containers. "What a lovely feast. Where is this from?"

"Sally's Salads downtown. One of my favorite places to eat. Oh, but don't touch the cake in the pan. It's not for us, sorry to say. I made it for May Fest and am dropping it off at church in the morning."

They said grace and forked some of the veggies. DiAne then peered at Wanda as she buttered her muffin. "So, tell me more about this shunning. I can see the worry on your face."

"Can you? Thought I had masked it well." Leave it to her friend to see through to the real her. She explained in more detail everything, including her theory about the kids staying at Aurora's. DiAne already knew the sorted past Wanda shared with the woman.

"But Todd told me this morning the police doubted Aurora had anything to do with this despite the fact their mother and Aurora were once sorority sisters."

"Hmmm. I brought my laptop. Between the two of us we could do a bit of digging."

Wanda set her soup spoon down. "Actually, there is another place I want to dig. I think this is not about me at all but someone is stirring the brew in that direction to divert attention." She leaned in. "I now wonder if perhaps the Clyburns are the real target."

"Why?"

Wanda told her about the incident right before they married when the newspaper office had been trashed and Tom conked unconscious.

"And the police never found the culprit?"

"Disappeared in the wind, as they say on those FBI shows." Wanda flit her fingers in the air.

DiAne's eyes sparkled. "Since Dick passed, I have been filling my evenings reading Christian fiction. No romance though. Too soon for that stuff. So, I have gotten into mysteries. Figured a few out before the end, too." She wiggled her eyebrows.

"Wait until you meet Evelyn next door! Oh, are you two ever going to get along."

"Good." She set her napkin on the table. "Then you can stay in the background and let us do the legwork. We'll get this solved by golly."

Wanda's mouth dropped open. Would it be possible? Had the calvary arrived?

CHAPTER 30

Evelyn came over that afternoon and for the first half hour Wanda may as well have left the room. The two chatted about mystery authors and books. DiAne had recently finished a series about mysteries mimicking famous nursery stories like *Cinderella* and *Jack in the Beanstalk*. "*A Giant Murder* by Marji Laine became my favorite. You should check them out."

"Are they in a boxed set? I really prefer paperback." Evelyn had three bookshelves filled with cozy mysteries.

"I think so."

As she listened to her friends and watched the excitement in their faces, Wanda wondered if she should start reading some as well. But right now, she wasn't sure reading mysteries would be a good diversion.

DiAne glanced over to her. "Well, it seems this town has a current mystery. How about we help our friend

Wanda figure it out?"

Evelyn's eyes danced then dimmed. "What about Todd? You don't want him to get into hot water. Didn't the chief practically ground you, Wanda?"

"Well . . ."

DiAne inched forward on the couch. "Actually, I think Wanda *should* stay out of it. People are suspicious already. But not of you. Especially not of me, a visitor."

Visitor. The answer to the next clue, the final clue. Wanda sucked in her breath. Had someone dumped iced sport drink over her like they did coaches? It felt as if they had, only on the inside. Her clothes remained dry. She shook the sensation away. It would come out on Tuesday after DiAne would be long gone.

"Wanda? You okay?"

She blinked and pressed her hand to her chest. "Yes. Just pondering."

Evelyn rubbed her hands together. "And . . . Whatcha think?"

"That I have wonderful friends. And Betty Sue would be hurt if we didn't ask her to join in."

Evelyn bobbed not just her head but her torso. "And perhaps Hazel. Scrub Oak Widows unite."

DiAne's melodic laugh danced over the room. "Oh, this is fun. Y'all should call it the Scrub Oak Widows' Society. You could abbreviate it the SOWS."

Evelyn chuckled as well. "More like Scrub Oak

Widow Sleuths."

The three scooted close enough to high-five.

W.

The five met over tea. Hazel brought roses for DiAne's bedside table along with a tin of British biscuits from the Coffee Bean. Evelyn whipped together some toast points with cream cheese and orange marmalade while Wanda and DiAne chopped apples and strawberries. Betty Sue brought celery sticks stuffed with pimento cheese. The first meeting of the SOWS, with an honorary member, began over afternoon tea.

Betty Sue spoke first. "Why would Aurora stir things back up almost two years later?"

"Revenge is a dish best served cold." Evelyn glanced around the room to each face.

Hazel shook a bony finger with a tad bit of garden dirt under the nail. She'd obviously been working in her rose beds. "No, no. I think someone didn't want Tom to retire and is trying to discredit Mason as an interloper. After all, these word puzzles started with Mason, correct?"

"Yes, they were his idea. He hired me." Wanda wiped her mouth. "You reckon someone doesn't want him to succeed?"

"Bingo." Hazel sat back, point made.

The other four studied each other's faces for a minute.

"She might be correct. Who are Tom's most loyal fans?" DiAne dug a notepad and pen from her purse, posed to write.

Maybe she should be a reporter. Wanda hid a grin.

Evelyn and Betty Sue answered in unison. "Everyone."

"Carol and Rollin are their best friends, but they are on a cruise together."

"Even if that is the case, how better to divert suspicion than to be out of the country, much less in the middle of the ocean?" DiAne tippy-tapped the end of her pen against her chin. "Who is this man and what do you know about him?"

"Tom? Only that he is about the most outstanding member in the community." Wanda sat back and folded her arms.

"And the other two?"

"Both Carol and Rollin go to my church. They are huge contributors." Evelyn harumphed. "In fact, he's a deacon. She leads the women's Bible study. No way would they be involved in anything illegal."

Betty Sue shrugged. "She's right."

All five pair of shoulders deflated a bit.

"How about a very loyal subscriber? Someone who doesn't care for change?" DiAne scanned the room for a response.

Hazel raised her hand. "Me and just about all the

people over fifty in Scrub Oak. Sorry, Wanda."

"No apologies needed. To be honest, though his programing is cleverly done, I prefer print as well."

DiAne chortled. "Sounds like my hometown. Why are we so resistant when life on this temporal sphere is all about change? Look at the seasons, the moon, and a baby that grows into a teen then an adult."

"True. Only God's love is eternal." Betty Sue averted her eyes briefly to the ceiling.

Evelyn snorted. "And people resist that more than anything."

Wanda cleared her throat. "Back to the subject at hand, ladies . . . who would be adamantly against Mason taking over as editor in chief or you, Wanda, being on staff?"

"Old man Baker. And you did embarrass him, Wanda." Betty Sue shrugged.

"Don't remind me." Wanda groaned. She swiveled to her guest. "He is the one I thought might be robbing people's identities but he was only digging in the trash cans for scraps for the feral cats he cares for."

"I do recall you telling me about it. But you two reconciled, right?"

"So, I thought. I have made that man so many casseroles and bought several flats of cat food from the mega discount store over the past few years."

Evelyn raised her voice volume to grab everyone's

attention. "The only way to find out is to chat up folk. Betty Sue, you and Hazel and I can do that, especially with May Fest gearing up. Ask casually how people are liking all the changes in the paper."

They nodded in agreement.

Being in charge for once suited Evelyn. Wanda could see it in her eyes. And this time, Wanda didn't mind taking a backseat. "What do you want DiAne and me to do?"

"DiAne. You keep Wanda company and try to dig up some background on Mason and or Vicki. Anything that may have angered someone and made them want to sabotage his success." Evelyn glanced around the room. "We'll meet again tomorrow after church before the May Fest activities kick off at one. Deal?"

The five shook hands. They chatted a bit more, and then parted with a mission assigned.

CHAPTER 31

Wanda and DiAne searched their laptops until their eyes crossed. Mason was presented as the golden child all over social media. Always the A student, an Eagle Scout, scholarship to Baylor for a degree in business management with a minor in commercial graphic arts, then to TCU for journalism. No mud ever stuck to him. Total Teflon.

"This guy is almost too good to be true, except we each have boys like him, right?" DiAne sat back and sipped her coffee.

"Right, and my nephew ranks high up there as well, that is until he arrested me." Wanda chuckled and stretched.

"I gather that was grandstanding, right? I mean no one at the station would ever think you to be behind these burglaries."

Wanda toggled her hand. "Until they have evidence to

state otherwise, I am still the number one suspect. Not that I committed them, mind you, but I could have hired someone to carry the burglaries out."

DiAne folded her arms. "Have they checked your bank account? In all these stories I read there is a lot of money withdrawn in a quick amount of time. Usually cash in small bills."

"Well, grocery prices have skyrocketed."

They both whooped. For Wanda it felt so good to have a hardy laugh. How long had it been? She so loved having her friend here. Particularly now.

DiAne wiped the corners of her eyes. "You want to don some sunglasses and wigs and go out to dinner? My treat."

"Absolutely not. You drove all the way here. It is my treat, and we will go with heads held high." She rose with her chin raised. "And all through dinner we will talk about how strong you are and how you toss bales of hay with one hand. And that turquoise is your favorite color and you love birds and antique necklaces. That'll give them fodder to gossip about."

DiAne slipped her sleeve above her bicep to show a tiny bump when she flexed. "Let's do this."

They decided on the Woods Grill that faced the lake on the south shore. As the two pulled into the parking lot, Wanda pointed. "There. See the roof line. That's Aurora's, the one for sale."

"Where the turquoise-soled college kids live?" DiAne turned to her. "I gather you'd like a table with a view of it?"

A slight grin spread over Wanda's lips. She couldn't help it. "Might be a dead end, but you never know."

The night had turned unexpectedly mild for approaching summertime in Texas. The ladies opted to eat outside on the back patio. The lights strung through the trees shimmered in the soft ripples of the black satiny lake distorting them into whipped stitches of gold. In the distance cicadas chirped.

Two other parties seated outside whispered their conversations, not so much about the two ladies seated across from them as to not disturb the serenity. Or so Wanda surmised from the fact their eyes never wandered in her direction.

One man did laugh and his voice carried on the sound waves. "I for one like the Hangman, but it is way too easy. I hope they get a bit harder."

DiAne winked. "See, not everyone is negative."

She swiveled out of her chair and walked over to the foursome.

What did she think she was doing? Wanda wanted to hide under the tablecloth.

"Excuse me. I'm new in town. But I am so impressed by your newspaper. It makes my hometown rag look like, well a limp rag." She giggled and they did as well. "Has it been around long?"

Here we go.

To Wanda's surprise they invited DiAne to sit with them. She couldn't catch all the conversation but it seems her out of town friend got quite the history lesson. Wanda scooted a bit closer while trying not to be obvious.

"But Tom's turned over the reins to his son-in-law. Guess I can't blame a man for wanting to slow it down a while. Especially after the injuries he sustained a while back."

They talked about the break in and the scandal of not finding the culprit that followed.

"Oh, my. And now that young man is running the show? Is that a good thing?"

DiAne definitely should become a reporter. People opened up to her the way they did Betty Sue, except DiAne didn't have *retired teacher* imprinted on her forehead. Before retiring, she had been a grief counselor. She knew how to draw people out and steer conversations.

The waiter brought their dinner, so she excused herself and returned to Wanda's table.

Wanda stabbed at her Caesar salad. "Glean anything?"

"Quite a bit, actually. I am glad you had your back to them, or I'm not sure they would have been so talkative. Three of the four admired Mason but believed most of the town felt there were too many changes too soon."

"Really? Anything in particular?"

She laid her hand on Wanda's shoulder. "No problems with the word puzzles other than, of course, the rash of robberies. Think they are fun and a good idea. Two had elementary-aged kids and they enjoyed the family time. Thought the interactive programing online to be pure genius."

"Good. That's Mason and Vicki's intent."

"And they like the emphasis of the reporting on the local events, awards and such. People get their national, state, and metro news elsewhere. It doesn't need to be repeated three days later in a twice-weekly newspaper."

"But . . ." So far it sounded as if Mason did a great job. However, Wanda sensed something else in DiAne's expression.

DiAne dabbed her mouth with the corner of her napkin. "But they felt as if Tom's legacy has been shoved out the door. They don't like the new header design or the font."

"Aw." She could understand. The original Old English lettering with the American flag fluttering through the word *Gazette* had become an icon. Mason had opted for a new design with blocked letters and a sketch of the town square gazebo offset to the left.

Could such a change in design spur someone to try and ruin its reputation? It seemed a tad extreme.

"You detected no sense of animosity toward me or Mason, though?"

"Never came up at all. They did seem concerned that the burglaries began when the digital edition started. They think a hacker from the dark web is involved."

"So did the police, but they brought in a county tech team who analyzed their office and home computers. They found no traces of either being hacked."

DiAne surveyed the lake for a few moments. "See how peaceful the water appears. Yet we do not know what lies below the surface. For all we know, a scuba diver could be drowning his victim."

"DiAne, maybe you should read another genre for a while."

She snickered. "What I mean is, I think this series of events are like the lake. The reason is swimming just below the surface. We can't quite view it yet. We need to figure out how to shine a light down into the depths. In fact, to give us time I have decided I can stick around for another day or so longer than anticipated, if you'll have me."

"Of course. Stay as long as you like."

Something about her friend's inner wisdom made Wanda hang on every word. Be it hope, or pure interest she didn't know. Then the image of Mason's car, submerged in that lake almost two years ago materialized in her mind. That's when he had been missing as well as the other reporter after Tom had been knocked out. What had occurred those five or six days before he wandered back into town dehydrated, disheveled, and confused?

"You may be right, dear friend. Mason and I are going to have a long talk on Monday morning. Now, let's finish our dinner and go watch a Rex Harrison movie."

Due to the circumstances, Betty Sue had dropped off the cake for Wanda before services while DiAne and Wanda chose to stay home and watch it on social media. The newly formed SOWS met in Wanda's living room after church. DiAne relayed her conversation with the party at the Wood Grill.

Evelyn agreed. "I talked to several people at the fellowship hour, and everyone thought the digital paper a brilliant way to engage the younger generation, but they were glad the Friday edition remained in print. No one seemed to have a grudge against Mason, though. They understood why Tom wanted to retire."

Hazel scooted forward in her chair. "Three people I spoke with expected Mason to change a few things, that always happens when someone takes the reins. But they missed the tried and true way the paper had been for decades. I didn't detect any animosity, though."

Just as Wanda suspected. "Well, then. I guess it must be something in either Mason's or Vicki's past." She turned to DiAne. "Guess we have to dig a bit deeper then.

But first, I want to talk with him tomorrow."

The meeting adjourned. As her friends left to enjoy the first afternoon of May Fest, Wanda's heart dipped. For the first time in over fifty years, she wouldn't participate. But for DiAne's sake she put on a brave face. After two games of Scrabble, they ordered barbeque sandwiches and chose another Rex Harrison movie to watch.

CHAPTER 32

Monday morning, Wanda glanced at the clock. Half-past-eight shouldn't be too early to make a call. She punched in Mason's number on her cell phone.

A woman's voice answered. Not one she recognized.

"I'm sorry, I thought I called Mason Clyburn."

"You did, my dear. They aren't here, though. I'm Mason's mother."

His mother? What was she doing there? Wanda introduced herself as working for the paper. "Is Mason available? It will only take a moment."

"Oh, dear, I'm sorry. Vicki and Mason are headed to the hospital. Her water broke two hours ago, so I hopped in my car and sped up here. Little Ian wants to come into the world a bit earlier than we expected."

Oh, dear was right. And Vicki's parents, Tom and Misty Jacobs, were on a cruise in the middle of the

Caribbean seas with Carol and Rollin Collins.

Forget snooping into his life. Obviously, his mind would not be on anything else than his wife and baby right now. Wanda texted Mason that he and Vicki were in her prayers and also to please let her know when Ian arrived in this world. She'd touch base later to see if she could be of help at *The Gazette.* Then she sent word through the prayer chain.

New birth always brought a sense of optimism. In a town of under a thousand residents, word would flow quickly. Perhaps, with God's good grace, attitudes about the newspaper would brighten. She could only hope.

DiAne padded in and made a beeline for the coffee. "What's got you grinning this early in the morning?"

Wanda told her about the pending arrival.

"Wow, earlier than expected, huh? I hope mother and baby will be all right. Guess your meeting with him is postponed then, huh?"

"It can wait."

Wanda called Todd, and they decided to give the Clyburns a month's worth of diaper service as a gift from the two of them. Then she invited him for breakfast while they waited for the news of Ian's arrival.

Todd appeared at the backdoor a little later with a sack. "Fresh berries from the Grocery Mart's organic section. Thought I'd contribute something to the meal."

Wanda took the basket and rinsed the fruit. She

actually hummed the hymn they often sang in church as she fixed breakfast.

DiAne came up alongside. "Smells good. You're humming, though. I don't think I have ever heard you hum."

"I have good reason to."

"Oh?"

"Today will be a great day. A new life will come into the world. And tomorrow will be even better."

"Why?" Todd and DiAne responded in unison.

"Because there will not be a Tuesday edition to *The Gazette*. Mason has too much on his hands. So, no puzzle, no crime."

W.

A cardinal must have chirped outside her window on Tuesday morning. She knew because the love-sick bird woke Sophie, who then proceeded to crawl across her head and put her front paws on the bedside table to peer out the window. The clock read fifteen until eight. Fine, may as well get up.

As the coffee brewed, Wanda noticed a text on her phone. *The Gazette* had arrived in her email. *What?*

She pulled up the webpage and shuddered. It comprised of three pages. The headlines read, *One more staff added to the newspaper: Ian Jacobs Clyburn, 6lbs*

14oz born at 12:32 p.m. Monday.

A brief account of the labor and birth sat underneath a photo of the three of them at the birthing bed. Vicki lay slightly upright with little Ian swaddled. Mason hovered with his arm across the back of the pillow, demonstrating what the saying *grinning from ear to ear* meant.

The inside pages consisted of advertisements, a list of May Fest events beginning that evening, and a quarter column of classified ads. She held her breath as she clicked to the back page. Yep, there appeared the word games and a good luck banner for the Scrub Oak baseball team.

Wanda groaned.

"What is it?" DiAne appeared in her robe with a yawn and her attention more on the gurgling coffee pot.

"The word puzzles showed up. Evidently Mason went to the newspaper office last night and whipped up an edition." Wanda rubbed her eyes. "I admire his sense of duty. *The Gazette* hasn't missed a deadline yet, even after the tornado of 1993 took out part of downtown."

DiAne peered over her shoulder. "What's the clue?"

Wanda showed her the cell phone screen. "I designed this puzzle weeks ago, long before I knew you'd be coming."

"A stranger to our town?"

Wanda waited a moment but the perplexed expression on DiAne face as she sipped her coffee didn't change.

236

"The answer starts with a 'v'."

"Visitor?"

Wanda nodded. "No one stole your jewelry in the night, did they?"

DiAne gasped. "My wedding ring set. And Grandma's pearls."

She dashed down the hall.

Wanda called out. "DiAne, I'm kidding. Come back and drink your coffee."

Then a screech bellowed down the hallway.

"N . . . No way." Wanda ran to the guest room. DiAne stood pointing at the dresser. Her hand shook and her breath labored.

"I put them right there. I know I did."

No, no, no. Oh, why had she disconnected the alarm system Todd nagged her to install? Because the fifty-second beeping until a code had been entered raised her blood pressure every time. She could never recall what had been preprogrammed. Three times the thing had blasted through the neighborhood. She knew she would develop PTSD from the ear-piercing noise and the fire department would fine her for another false alarm, so she attacked the wires with her sewing scissors. But she'd left the sign in the front yard and the sticker on the kitchen window as a deterrent. Guess that idea hadn't worked.

Even so, Wanda held hope. Surely nobody would sneak in and rob her home? "They have to be around here.

I'll check the bathroom. You go through your suitcase."

Tears shimmered in her friend's eyes but she obeyed without saying a word.

After a half hour of turning over everything that they could from sofa cushions to the bedding to the trash baskets, the two gave up.

"Now what do we do?" DiAne moaned as she reached for a tissue from the box on the sofa table.

Wanda's blood boiled. How dare someone invade her home and rob her friend? Stealing a new widow's wedding set ranked up there with butchering puppies and drowning kittens.

"I'm calling Todd. I don't care if I wake him up."

He arrived ten minutes later. By then DiAne had run out of tears, and Wanda had been depleted of Kleenex. Wanda briefly explained everything up to that point.

"I'm afraid we searched the house from rafter to subfloor. Any fingerprints left behind we probably compromised. I didn't think."

"Come outside a minute."

The quiet sternness of his voice disturbed her. So did the look in his eye. He led her through the backyard gate around to the front. Did he plan on dragging her to jail? She willed her feet to follow him.

He halted as he rounded to the front yard and pointed.

Wanda opened her mouth to scream but nothing came out.

On one of the main branches of her oak tree, suspended from a hangman's noose, dangled a pair of turquoise-soled sneakers and a note pinned to the laces that read, "I solved your puzzle. Too bad you didn't solve mine."

Julie B Cosgrove

CHAPTER 33

Wanda wrapped her robe tighter around her and tried to ignore the growing crowd of neighbors pointing and whispering out of her hearing range.

"Well, the good news is, I guess this exonerates me." She stared at the effigy slightly swaying in the morning breeze.

Todd shifted his weight, his arms crossed over his chest. "Unless you hung this up yourself and stole your friend's jewelry to divert attention from yourself."

Her mouth flew open. Then she saw the tiny laugh lines at the edge of his eyes lengthen.

"Todd Martin. Sometimes I wish I could still turn you over my knee."

"Actually, as a cop I need to consider all the angles. However, that is definitely not your handwriting. Nor your shoes."

"And how did you determine that?"

He pointed at the pair of shoes dangling by the laces. "For one they are a size six and you wear eights, correct?"

Now how did he know that? Had he snooped in her closet? Then she recalled her house shoes she kept by the backdoor to slip into in case Sophie needed to go outside and had once again opted to not use her doggie door. Sometimes Wanda figured the mutt wanted supervision, or company. Not that she could blame her. We all need someone to tell us "good girl" and pat us on the head every now and then. The idea that Todd had noticed the size in the soles did impress her though. He'd make a great detective one day.

Her thoughts returned to her nephew's explanation. "See how they have small scuffs near where the little toes would lie? And the turquoise is a bit lighter on the ball of the sole. Plus, though the size is stamped in the left one it is almost illegible. Definitely broken in. Not newly purchased."

"Very good, Todd. They did teach you something at the academy."

He side-glanced at her.

"No, I mean it. I am impressed." She pressed her hand to her throat. "If that came out harsh, I apologize. I'm in a nasty mood right now."

He patted her shoulder blade. "Can't blame you. Unfortunately, I have to leave this sign hanging up. Need to dust for prints, yah-dah, yah-dah. Cordon it off, too."

"I understand." It didn't mean she liked the idea of making her front lawn a crime scene.

By that time DiAne had joined them. Wanda heard her soft gasp.

Todd turned to her. "DiAne, if you don't mind, I would like to fingerprint you for purposes of elimination. I already have my aunt's on file."

Wanda rolled her eyes. Thank goodness DiAne didn't ask why. Instead, she whispered her consent.

Todd gave her a sympathetic smile. "Let me call this in. You two return to the kitchen. I'll join you ladies inside in a bit and go over the events of this morning with you one more time."

"I'll put some more coffee on." Wanda waved to her neighbors, which made a few of them turn away. Head held high, she walked inside the front door DiAne had exited from moments before.

She stood at the kitchen counter, hands grasping the tile edges as she watched the coffee machine gurgle and drip. She enjoyed her pod machine, but when brewing for company she still used the one with the glass carafe. Besides, the rhythmic sound soothed her nerves at the moment.

"What are you thinking about?"

DiAne's voice jolted her. Wanda let out an elongated sigh from deep down in her gut.

"I am so, so sorry I invited you to stay with me while this . . . whoever she is . . ." She waved her hand in the air. ". . . is still raking havoc. If I hadn't, your jewelry would be safe and sound."

Her friend wrapped her arm around Wanda's shoulders. "Don't go blaming yourself."

Wanda felt the anger build behind her eyes. "I knew the answer to the last clue but figured Mason would wait until Friday to publish it. Not today as a special edition. By then you'd be long gone. No longer a visitor."

DiAne twisted Wanda to face her. "That's it!"

Todd's boots shuffled across the kitchen floor. "What?"

"Who else besides Mason would know he'd decide to go ahead and post an edition today so soon after his first son arrived?"

Her nephew and she stared at each other for a second and shrugged.

Wanda responded first. "I guess Vicki would. But she's kinda preoccupied right now."

Todd chuckled. "Yeah, I think we can safely rule her out."

DiAne nodded. "Agreed. Who else?"

Wanda's mind went blank. DiAne's eyes widened as if to coax her answer, but none surfaced.

Todd slapped his forehead. "Tom. Mason would have called Tom and Misty to let them know they needed to end the cruise early. I imagine Tom persuaded him to put the edition out."

"Bingo." DiAne gave him a thumb's up signal.

Wanda felt her legs wobble. She slid into one of the kitchen dinette chairs. "Whoa. Wait. You think Tom is sabotaging Mason's taking over the paper? He wanted to retire. He's never fully recovered from being assaulted, still gets fierce headaches, and his concentration has suffered. Besides, he's been gone."

"No, I don't think so. From the way those people described him at dinner he'd almost qualify for sainthood." DiAne smirked, then her face muscles tightened. "However, that paper made up his whole life. Well, besides his family, right? Letting go wouldn't be an easy thing. I imagine he and Mason communicated before each edition hit the stands."

Wanda felt dense as four-inch plywood. "Then who?"

"Someone who knew them well enough to know they would communicate and also knew their cell phone numbers."

"To what end?"

Her nephew snapped his fingers. "To hack into their conversations. It wasn't Mason's computer we needed to monitor but his and Tom's phones." Todd's voice became hurried as his eyes gleamed. "I need to let the chief know. Brilliant, DiAne."

"Reading those mysteries have given me a mindset I

guess." She tapped her temple.

Wanda tried to keep up. "You mean anyone can listen in on conversations?"

Todd tilted his head and grinned at her naivety the way a father about to explain aerodynamics to his three-year-old would. "Like everything else, my dear aunt, there's an app for that. Several in fact."

"That's disconcerting. Isn't it illegal?"

He puffed through his cheeks.

"Never mind." Wanda didn't want to know. "So how do we find out?"

"*We* don't Aunt Wanda. This is a police matter. I'll call the county tech guys and ask them to check it out. But first I need to ask Mason and Tom if they have noticed an increased drainage of batteries, any unusual background reception, a lag in their phones disconnecting, etcetera." He walked toward the backdoor.

"Weren't you going to go over this morning with us?" Somehow having Todd there made Wanda feel safer.

"Later. This takes priority. I'll see if Reagan or Jimmy Bob can come by."

He gave her an empathetic smile as love emitted from his eyes. "Take care. And stay home today, all right? Except, try not to touch anything in the guest room anymore, just in case."

DiAne laced her arm around Wanda's elbow. "We have several more Rex Harrison movies to keep our minds off things. We'll be fine."

Todd chuckled and left.

Wanda patted DiAne's hand. "I take it all back. I am very glad you are here, dear friend."

"Me, too. My spirits are lifted. Something tells me Todd will find my jewelry soon." She gave Wanda a warm smile. "How about *Dr Doolittle*? I don't feel like watching one of Rex' mysteries."

"Deal. But maybe we should both get dressed first and try to eat some breakfast. I have a feeling this will be Grand Central Station today."

"Good idea." DiAne giggled and went to her room to change clothes. When she reached the door, she turned back to Wanda. "I'll be careful what I touch, though I've already turned the room upside down."

Would finding fingerprints after a thorough search by two ladies count as a miracle? *If you don't mind, God, and if it isn't too much to ask . . .*

Julie B Cosgrove

By the time Dr. Doolittle and company had set sail to find the giant pink snail, Evelyn and Betty Sue appeared at the door. Soon after that, Fred arrived with shortbread cookies from the import store in Fort Worth. Wanda didn't ask how he knew. But the rose in Betty Sue's cheeks when he arrived told her he'd been the first person she'd called. The twinkle in his eyes as they landed on Betty Sue's face told Wanda he was one smitten guy.

Then Reagan arrived in order to interview Wanda and DiAne while everyone else politely listened as they sipped coffee and dunked cookies.

"Neither of you recall hearing anything?"

DiAne shook her head.

Wanda sat straighter. "Wait. Sophie woke me up walking across my head. She put her paws on my bedside table and peered at the window, growling. I thought she talked to the cardinal chirping outside in the tree. Maybe she saw or heard someone on the driveway."

Reagan wrote it down. "About what time?"

"Seven forty-five. That is what my digital clock read. I set it three minutes ahead so I am not late to things. So, I guess the real time would have been seven forty-two."

The policewoman nodded as she jotted the information down.

Wanda and DiAne both went through their movements, including searching for the jewelry.

"We probably wrecked any chance of you lifting a strange set of prints, right?"

"You never know. I brought a portable kit. Mrs. Gates, would you be so kind?"

Betty Sue jumped to her feet. "I'll get a dishtowel. Don't want black stuff on the carpet."

Reagan flashed her a soft grin. "Actually, it is all digital now."

Oh." Betty Sue's cheeks blushed as she returned to her place on the couch.

"Like at the DMV? I had my thumbs imprinted there." DiAne volunteered. "Can you access those?"

"Yes. But a full set would be ideal."

She held up all ten fingers and wiggled them. "Let's do it, then."

After that, DiAne contacted her insurance company. They promised to email the description of her jewelry to the police station. "Thank goodness Dick insisted we take out that extra policy years ago."

Reagan rose and nodded to the TV. Frozen on the screen due to them pausing the movie, the crew set out with Dr Doolittle and his parrot on their sea adventure. "Love that movie. Watch it with my nieces when they come to visit."

Everyone in the room bobbed their head in agreement.

After the policewoman searched for fingerprints, took pictures, then left, Evelyn turned to Wanda. "What do we do now?"

Wanda sat back in her recliner and flipped up the footrest. "Finish watching the movie, I guess."

Betty Sue came over and felt her forehead. "What? Not sneaking off to sleuth? Call the police back in here. An alien invasion has occurred." She bent closer to eye Wanda's face. "Who are you and what did you do with my friend Wanda?"

"Oh, stop. I'm fine. Todd told us to stay put, that's all."

"And you are complying? I changed my mind. Someone call 9-1-1." Betty Sue faked shock as she raised her hand to her forehead.

Evelyn cackled.

DiAne snickered.

Fred shook his head. "I will leave you ladies, then. If you need anything . . ."

"Thanks, Fred. We'll let you know. Promise." Wanda sat forward as the recliner's footrest plopped back into place. "Appreciate the cookies."

He waved and left out the backdoor. Wanda couldn't help but notice Betty Sue's smile lessened a bit as she watched him leave.

"Are we really gonna do nothing?" Evelyn's face drooped.

"DiAne basically solved the case." Wanda gave her friend a silent applause. "All we have to do is wait for Todd and the county techies to follow through."

"Oh, pooh." DiAne shifted her eyes to her feet as the others congratulated her. "Sometimes it takes a fresh pair of eyes. Wanda, you were too close to the situation."

Suddenly a large KABOOM sounded from the kitchen.

Everyone screamed.

Wanda ran through the dining room as the smoke billowed through the doorway. She coughed as she fanned away the clouds to see what happened.

Her stove gaped open as if in shock. The oven door had been blown across the room and the dinette set toppled like children's blocks.

"Sophie!" Wanda's heart shot into her tonsils.

A muffled whimper answered her. A small brown, floppy-eared head appeared from inside the pantry.

Thank goodness she had left the door open after

searching for some sugar to put in the bowl for the guests' coffees.

Wanda scooped her pet onto her lap, tears streaming down her cheeks. She examined Sophie for any bleeding.

"Is she all right?" DiAne bent down as well.

"Think so." Wanda checked the paws.

The dog nuzzled into the crook of her master's arm.

Wanda stroked her back and scanned the charred room. "Well, looks like someone figured out the main answer to the Hangman puzzle."

Evelyn and Betty Sue responded in unison. "*An oven.*"

Wanda nodded then broke down in sobs.

Betty Sue dialed Todd's number. "You need to get over here. Now!"

Julie B Cosgrove

CHAPTER 35

Sirens, firemen, police, and a small crowd of neighbors gathering at the curb for a second time that day filled Wanda's world for the next half hour. She tried her hardest to put on a positive face, but as the day dragged, her efforts waned.

Jay King sat with her at the dining room table. He calmly and quietly went through the insurance papers and estimate to get her kitchen back in order. "I'll call in some favors, not that I have to. People know you."

"That obviously is not a good thing." She tried to end the sentence in a small laugh and failed miserably.

"It will take about six to eight weeks to repair the damage. But the policy will cover it after your $500 deductible."

Betty Sue grabbed her fingers. "Well, you've been wanting a new kitchen for years but never knew how to afford it."

Jay arched an eyebrow.

Betty Sue stumbled over her words. "Oh, that's not what I meant. I mean . . . I'm sure Wanda wouldn't ever . . . I mean . . ."

He chuckled. "I know. And I will emphasize that point to the home office."

Wanda's temples began to press together as if her head had been shoved into one of those automatic jar openers, the curved arms slowly tightening and twisting until a pop sounded.

She sighed and turned to DiAne. "Well, visits with me cannot be described as dull."

"You do go to extremes to keep people entertained." She winked. "Aspirin?"

"Please." Wanda dipped her head and massaged both sides of her face above the cheekbones until they felt warm.

"Do you need to go to the hospital, Aunt Wanda?" Todd's voice sounded shaky.

"No, dear boy. Just a pounding headache. Tension. I'm fine." He'd bent to her level so she reached over and kissed his cheek. "We were all in the living room when it happened. How could someone have sneaked in? Reagan sat right over there."

"Didn't have to." Chief Archer peeked into the dining room with his fire helmet's shield tilted back. He held up a charred timer.

Todd rose. "Let me see that thing." He donned plastic gloves and held it by the wires, examining it. "Did you use the oven this morning?"

"No, we made cheese, green pepper, and sausage omelets on the stove. And made toast in the toaster." Wanda felt a shiver jolt through her. "You mean if I had decided to bake muffins it could have blown up in our faces?"

"Not necessarily. It's set for eleven-thirty in the morning. Interesting time."

DiAne returned with the aspirin bottle and a glass of water to set by Wanda. "So, if we had been fixing lunch . . ."

Wanda shook her head then regretted the action. It worsened the throbbing. "It's too hot to heat up the kitchen for lunch. It's nearing summertime in Texas for goodness' sake."

"Maybe whoever did this figured you'd be out of the house for May Fest stuff today?" Betty Sue glanced around the room, her expression seeking affirmation. "It wasn't meant to harm you, just scare you."

"She may be onto something." Todd leaned against the door jamb that separated the burnt kitchen from the dining room and the rest of the front of the house. "The sign warned us. The perp had solved the puzzle. That didn't mean today's clue but the whole thing. The six clues spelled *A-N-O-V-E-N*."

"But why steal DiAne's jewelry?"

"Why steal things from the merchants? A thief is a thief. They rarely morph into murderers unless it is to conceal their theft."

"I agree." Chief Archer slipped the timer into an evidence bag for Todd. "This detonator is designed to cause an explosion but not a deadly one."

Todd slipped his thumbs into his belt. "So, whoever is behind this, he or she didn't want you killed."

"She." Wanda and Betty Sue answered at the same time.

Betty Sue grinned at their habit to answer alike. "Anne Graves and Gloria Longoria both are certain they were attacked by a female."

Wanda swallowed two aspirin with a swig of water then leaned back in her chair. "Make that a young, athletic female, perhaps with dark hair who wears turquoise . . ."

Todd's face lost all color. "Dark-haired? Are you sure?"

Wanda eyed Betty Sue. "Yeah. When we interviewed them together, that is what they said, right?"

"Think so." Betty Sue shrugged.

"I thought she was a blonde?" Todd rubbed his forehead.

"Well, that attorney's granddaughter is, I guess. But I thought maybe the ski mask had them confused."

"The black and white mask per your report." Todd gazed at her.

"Yeah, per Gloria. But not really black and white, mostly black with a white trim. Though Anne said the one who whacked her wore a red and white one. You know, the kind that has stylized deer knitted into the rim."

"I don't recall that in the report." His eyelids narrowed as he swallowed hard. "You're sure now? Black with white trim for one. Red and white with deer for the other?"

"And dark bangs. Positive. Why?"

Todd didn't answer. Instead, he dashed from the house.

Julie B Cosgrove

CHAPTER 36

"Where did he go?" Wanda scanned the dining room and into the living room across the hallway from the front door.

"I'll follow him." Evelyn got up to leave.

"Let me go with you." DiAne stood and grabbed her purse from the peg on the wall in the hallway.

They've become fast friends." Betty Sue snickered.

"Cozy mysteries. Quite a bond." Wanda sighed.

From the bay window in the dining room, Wanda watched the two skedaddle across the lawn as Todd's cruiser pulled away. A few seconds later, Wanda heard Evelyn's car engine rev and craned to observe her back out of the driveway between their houses. DiAne slid into the passenger seat and off they went as the neighbors gawked and whispered to each other. Wanda momentarily thought about charging admission to cover her deductible.

"I think the aspirin is kicking in, thanks Betty Sue." She focused on her agent who had been sitting quietly with a perplexed expression. "Jay, so tell me. Can I stay here during the repairs or do I need to vacate the premises?"

He shrugged. "You could stay I guess, but you won't have a kitchen for at least a month or so."

"Maybe we could take that road trip we've talked about." Betty Sue scooted up in her chair. "There's four-day Christian women's conference coming up in West Monroe. It's only a four hour drive. We could see if they have a last minute registration."

Wanda jutted out her lower lip. "It's an idea. Maybe Evelyn and Hazel would go with us. We could take my sedan. It's bigger."

"And pick up DiAne on the way. Three can fit in the back. I really like her."

Wanda genuinely smiled for the first time that day. "SOWS unite."

As they laughed, she noticed Jay King giving them another perplexed expression. Poor man probably felt as out of place as a mouse in a house of cats.

Wanda explained the acronym.

"Aw. I see. Clever." He didn't seem convinced, but he stacked his papers and shoved them into a folder. "Well, ladies. I will be in touch. And Wanda, we have a guest room and bath. You're more than welcome—"

She grasped his hand in a firm shake. "That is so

sweet of you to offer. I know Kathy wouldn't mind either. But Evelyn has the same, and I think I'd rather be next door to keep an eye on things, at least the first few weeks."

"Understood. But the offer still stands if you change your mind."

As he closed the door behind him, Wanda's phone pinged. Evelyn sent a text. *Lost him.*

Oh, well. Patience is the virtue God kept trying to teach her. Time for another lesson, then. She'd find out sooner or later.

The fire fighters cleared out as well. The house now seemed strangely quiet except for Sophie scratching on the bedroom door. Poor pooch.

Wanda tiptoed into what was left of the kitchen, found the doggie bowls, and scrubbed them vigorously. Then she filled one with kibbles and the other half-way with water and carried them to her bedroom. Betty Sue followed with the doggie bed she'd sponged clean and hung to dry in the sun while the firemen crawled all over the place and the police wound yellow tape around the area.

"Thanks for doing that, by the way. It never entered my brain."

"You had enough on your mind, Wanda. It needed doing and I needed something to do."

Wanda understood. She eased open her bedroom door. "Here, girl. Looks like you are going to be confined for a while. Sorry."

The dog peered at her with mournful brown eyes as she set down the food. Betty Sue laid the doggie bed near the foot of Wanda's queen-sized one.

Wanda stood and watched as Sophie lapped water. "Who would do this? And why?" She clenched her fists digging her nails into her palms. She wanted to hit something, scream, or curl up in a ball and suck her thumb—maybe all three.

"If we knew that, we'd figure out their identity."

Wanda sat on the bed and pulled her knees to her chin. "I honestly thought DiAne had hit on something. The phone tapping. Learning the clues that way. Trying to discredit either Mason or Tom or *The Gazette* in general. But today . . . Now I don't know. It's personal again." She buried her head in her hands.

She felt the mattress dip and Betty Sue's lavender and vanilla scent whiff next to her. Then her friend's hand rubbed small circles on her upper back the way Wanda's own mother used to when Wanda had a skinned knee or later a broken teenage heart. And the way Wanda did with her own daughter Wesley all those times. A gesture of comfort handed down from one generation of women to the next.

After a cleansing sigh, she raised her head. "Who hates me, Betty Sue?"

Her friend's eyes shimmered. "I honestly cannot think of a soul, dear. I really can't, which is why we're all so baffled."

Wanda swiped her lower eyelids and stared out her bedroom window. "What did you see, Soph? Oh, how I wish you could talk."

The dog cocked her head and then continued lap her water.

Julie B Cosgrove

An hour later, Wanda sat at the dining room table tapping the end of a pen as she stared at the note pad in front of her. Her friends had gathered around her for support. DiAne and Evelyn had stopped off and gotten cups of coffee from the Coffee Bean as well as pastries and fresh fruit since Wanda's kitchen wasn't really a kitchen anymore.

"Okay, we know Aurora is not fond of me." She wrote the name. "And we know the Dallas attorney who is buying her place is a friend of hers. Her grandkids mysteriously arrived to spruce up the place for dear old granny, or so they told Henry. That seems a bit unrealistic."

Betty Sue, Evelyn, and DiAne gave her blank expressions.

Wanda continued. "One of them had turquoise-soled

athletic shoes and they are the right age. Henry thought they appeared fit. But they had blonde hair, not dark. I had forgotten about that detail."

"A wig?" Evelyn offered the suggestion with her palms up.

DiAne wagged her finger. "Then why wear a ski mask that covers most of the hair anyway?"

"To cover their face. Maybe one has a chicken pox scar, a beauty mark, acne, or some other telltale feature."

"Possibly, Ev. Good thinking." Wanda dialed Hardware Haven and put Henry on speaker mode so the ladies could hear. "Henry here's a weird question. Those kids that bought all the materials to fix up Aurora's old place. Did either of them have a distinct mark on their faces? A scar, or maybe bad acne or a mole?"

"What's this about?" His tone sounded suspicious.

"Well, believe it or not you seem to be the only one who has actually seen them. I mean, we may have, but we only have a vague description. They are both blondes, right?"

"Yeah, and tall. Thin. But fit like they work out or run or something. Faces? Hmmm. The girl, I think her name is Avery, she does have a dark mole on her lower lip. The boy is Mick or Nick. He is quiet. A few acne scars on the cheeks, but not readily noticeable. He is trying to grow a beard, though. Either that or has given up shaving. Hard tell the first few weeks when they're a blonde."

"Thanks, now if we see them about town, we can introduce ourselves. I've gone twice to take them a newcomer packet but they never seem to be there."

"Oh, okay. Say, I heard about your kitchen. Bad stove, huh? Gas leaks can be dangerous."

"Yes, so they can." Wanda eyed her friends. *So, that's the story that's being spread around?*

"You know I will give you a discount on supplies, paint, you name it."

"Thanks, Henry. That is sweet of you."

He chuckled. "Well, it is always sweet of you to buy something in my store even if you didn't come in for anything more than to glean info. You care about your town and most of us care about you."

She felt her cheeks warm. "That's good to know, Henry. Thanks. And I will let Jay know about your kind offer. He is handling the estimates."

"Then you're in good hands. Take care. Bye."

She hung up. "Well, ladies. Thoughts?"

Betty Sue raised her hand. "If they are strangers, why the masks? It isn't as if anyone would know them."

DiAne pointed at her. "Exactly why they would. Like mine, this is a small community where everyone knows everyone else. Strangers stand out like spots on a zebra."

Everyone laughed.

Betty Sue frowned. "I have a hard time believing Aurora could orchestrate all of this from afar, wherever she is."

Evelyn huffed. "Yeah, she's probably too busy trying to snare hubby number four."

Wanda snickered. "True. Plus, a high-powered Dallas lawyer wouldn't risk her reputation, retiring or not, by getting her grandkids involved in crime for revenge's sake. Silly of me to think like that. This isn't one of those un-reality TV series on cable."

Everyone agreed.

"Who else hates me?"

"The Ferguson heirs?" Evelyn shrugged.

"I don't think so, Ev. Pat Farmer wouldn't have purchased that place and renovated it into a B&B if we hadn't uncovered some of its savory history. No, I think they'd be thanking me."

"Mr. Baker likes your casseroles too much and besides he is not tech savvy." Betty Sue flicked a piece of kitchen ash from the tabletop. "He's out."

"You were kidnapped last year." DiAne raised her eyebrows a tad.

"Only for twenty minutes or so. Didn't press charges. A misunderstanding." Wanda groaned and rose. "I want comfort food. A cheeseburger. Chocolate milkshake. Fries."

"I'll go get it." Evelyn stood. "I'm starved."

Everyone threw money on the table as Wanda wrote down their orders—even health-conscious and fitness buff

Betty Sue. "Got to cheat every now and then."

Forty minutes later the foursome pulled away from the table patting bellies. "So much for those thirty pounds I've lost. I think they found me again." Wanda exhaled a long breath.

DiAne slapped her hand to her thigh. "I knew you'd lost a lot. You really do look great."

"Betty Sue encouraged me. She's lost, what? Fifty-two now?"

"Fifty-four." She blushed.

All clapped and Betty Sue stood to take a bow then sat back down and slurped loudly the last of her strawberry shake through the straw.

Hoots and whistles echoed through the room. Stress relief and junk food were therapeutic things sometimes.

But Wanda felt her chest tighten again. They were no closer to solving who did this than this morning. Her kitchen remained a charred shamble. An effigy of her word puzzle creation hung in her front yard, and five townsfolks had been burgled.

And where had Todd dashed off to? And why had he not been in touch?

Something didn't quite fit.

Julie B Cosgrove

CHAPTER 38

Wanda glanced at the mantle clock. A little after eight already. She peeked through her blinds into the quiet dusk and then turned them closed.

"Are we keeping you up?" DiAne's tone sounded playful.

"No, it's just that . . . well I feel antsy. I want to get in there and scrub the floors, or the countertops. Something." She slumped into the sofa cushions.

"I remember when our house flooded." Evelyn came and sat on the couch with Wanda.

"I never knew that. How old were you?"

"Sixteen. My sister thirteen. A major storm came through and dumped five inches of rain into the creek. The water got halfway up the sides of the rooms, about the height of the wainscotting. We waded through it grabbing what we could. It came up so fast we barely had time to get the family Bible and our photo albums out. I recall having to leave my teddy bear I'd had most my life. I later found him floating face down as if he'd drowned. We hung him in the tree to dry. He stank to high heavens after three days. Dad burned him along with a lot of our stuff that had been ruined. I still remember staring into that fire as we all wept."

DiAne and Betty Sue gathered around to listen.

Evelyn took Wanda's hand. "You feel helpless, Wanda. Just as we did until the water receded. It took two and a half days. But there is a light at the end of the darkness. We got to design our house again because so many walls had to be knocked down. I got a much better bedroom. You're getting a new kitchen."

"Yes, I suppose. Maybe I can get excited about that in a few days." She scanned the concerned faces huddled near her. "Thank you all for helping me set up a temporary one in the dining room and getting what dishes and glasses didn't break washed in the bathtub."

"At least the firemen helped move the fridge in here. My muscles would be screaming now if we tried." DiAne pressed the small of her hand to her lower back.

"Where *did* Todd go? He didn't stay to help at all?" Evelyn harumphed.

"That's what's got me antsy. It's been over ten hours, and I have no idea where he is or what he is doing much less why he dashed out of here." Wanda rested her chin in her hand, balanced by her elbow propped on one of the sofa arms.

"Call him." DiAne handed her the cell phone.

Wanda started to but changed her mind. "He's on duty. May Fest is in full swing. He's probably swamped with traffic patrol." Her thumbs moved over the tiny QWERTY board on the phone. "I'll text him and ask him to call when he has a chance."

"Be sure to reiterate that you're fine, and nothing else bad has happened." Evelyn pointed to the screen.

Wanda did. Then she slapped her forehead. "I never got in touch with Mason. What is wrong with my brain?"

"Well, you had a frightful morning. Someone broke in, stole DiAne's jewelry, hung a nasty note on your tree, then your oven blew up . . ." Betty Sue's eyes rolled to the ceiling as she counted on her fingers. "Besides, I imagine he has his hands full right now. Call him tomorrow."

"You're right." Wanda set her phone down on the coffee table.

"Are you two bunking out here tonight?" Evelyn's eyes danced between Wanda and DiAne.

"I can't answer for my guest here, but I want to stay. Poor Sophie has been through enough. She needs me. Her life will be topsy turvy enough in the weeks to come."

DiAne yawned. "I'm fine to stay. The odor isn't that bad now. A hot soak in that wonderful tub of yours, a chapter or two of Philippians, and a goodnight's sleep is the ticket. I suggest the same for you, dear hostess. Things will seem better in the morning."

"No Rex Harrison?"

She uncurled her legs from underneath her. "Thanks, Wanda. But not tonight. You understand?"

"I do. I get the tub after you."

Betty Sue rose. "That's our cue to skedaddle, Ev. Could you drive me home? My legs are too exhausted to walk."

"Sure." She turned to Wanda and DiAne. "We'll see you both later. I'll bring you breakfast in the morning about eight, okay? Holler if you need anything before then."

Her friends left and her guest went to run the water in the bathroom.

Wanda stared at the note pad, clucked her teeth, and wadded up the top sheet. Not Aurora, then. Not Mr. Baker. Not the Fergusons. Then who? *Who?*

And why had Todd not texted her back?

A knot in the middle of her stomach began to cinch once again.

Her guest may relax in a hot tub and then turn in, but Wanda had the suspicion she'd be up pacing the floor until he responded.

The mantle clock struck nine.

She pulled up *The Gazette* website. She scanned May Fest events schedule. Finals over, the graduating students' lock-in began now. The middle school's play would have ended. Ah, and the fireworks in the town square would start in thirty minutes after the Cleburne Choir finished singing in the Gazebo. That's where Todd would be.

Wanda used a refreshing toner to remove the last bit of soot from her face and applied some fresh makeup. Then she changed into jeans and the Scrub Oaks T-shirt Mayor Arnold had designed for the event. She slipped into her comfortable loafers and scribbled a note to DiAne.

"Restless. Going to watch the fireworks in the square. See you in the morning."

She placed it on DiAne's suitcase sitting on the guest bed, grabbed her house keys, and began to walk toward the festive sounds in the distance.

When she entered downtown, Wanda gawked at the huge crowd. Not only did most of Scrub Oak turn out but people from the neighboring towns as well. So much for the robberies deterring any of the festivities.

She scanned the square, looking for Todd's Stetson. There were too many heads blocking her view, even when she stood on tiptoe. So, she bought a bottle of water at a vendor booth and began to meander.

"He has to be here somewhere." She muttered it to herself, though no one could have heard her over the music anyway. The choir was not dressed in robes but in white slacks and fuchsia shirts. They sang a hip-hop version of *God Bless America*. Not her taste, but people were clapping to it. Whatever. Back in her day her elders balked at Jimmy Hendrick's rendition of the National Anthem.

She inched sideways through a group of folks to avoid their elbows and hopped up on the stone ledge that made a horseshoe shape around the gazebo. Craning her head, she observed the crowd.

No Todd. Feeling the frustration bubble up in her, she went to step down to the sidewalk when something caught her eye. Two blonde heads slightly higher than most of the patrons. A guy and a girl. Could it be?

The girl turned her head. Yes, the lights hanging above the square illuminated her face enough for Wanda to see the dark mole near her mouth. Avery. She'd found them.

Now, not to lose them. Wanda snaked through the mass of humanity keeping an eye on the siblings. Maybe they had nothing to do with the robberies. Perhaps they'd never actually met Aurora even if their mom knew her. Still, something about them didn't sit right with Wanda. Her gut sent out warning signs.

She decided she'd find out why, and if she ran into Todd in the process, good. Two mysteries solved.

Chapter 39

As she wound her way through the mob of laughing and clapping people, Wanda saw the two siblings veer off to the right and walk up 7th Street toward the police station. Why would they be going there?

She got her answer. They weren't. A few seconds later, they crossed the street and continued toward the lower school property that housed both the elementary and middle schools. The streetlamps cast a golden glow over the road but the sidewalks were shadowed by the trees lining the curbs. Wanda had to wait until her eyes refocused to follow them.

As the din of the crowd began to fade, she could hear them talking to each other. Avery had her hands to her side, but the boy's, Mick or Nick, became animated. His tone sounded hurried though they were too far away for Wanda to pick up specific words.

Avery halted and turned to him. Her body language indicated displeasure as if she chewed him out. Then she threw her hair off her shoulder and strutted ahead of him.

He picked up the pace to catch up to her.

What had that been about? Wanda stayed to the shadows and walked flatfooted to avoid them hearing her loafer heels hit the concrete. Oh, why had she not worn her Zumba tennis shoes?

Up ahead, she saw the school parking lot. A few cars still dotted it, most likely volunteers cleaning up after the play.

The two crossed cattycornered at Cedar Drive and walked along the chain link fence toward the entrance to the lot on 8th Street. Wanda stopped and crouched behind a huge oak trunk. She'd figured they'd turn in the opposite direction, walk past Holy Hill Church, and continue up 6th Street to Aurora's house. But they didn't. They entered the school grounds.

Why would they stop there?

Avery froze just for a moment and turned her torso to gaze back down the street. Did she detect Wanda following them? People sometimes had a sense about things.

Wanda slid further behind the tree.

A screech assaulted Wanda's ears. An owl hooted and fluttered from the branches, nearly making her jump out of her skin. She crammed her fist in her mouth to stop the startled gasp that would give her position away. Her heart thumped inside her ears as she took four deep breaths through her nose to calm her rattled nerves.

"Whoa, look at that!" The boy must have seen the giant bird.

"So what? Let's go, Nick. We're late." Avery's voice echoed down the street, her tone irritated.

Late? For what? The play ended almost an hour ago. At least now she knew his name for real. Wanda dared to peek from her hiding place. Good. They walked on, their backs to her. No other pedestrians could be seen.

Thunk. Swish. Boom. The sky lit in blue and red. Then a burst of sparkling rays appeared and filtered down through the tree limbs. The fireworks had begun.

Oohs and aahs from the people in the square fluttered on the breeze. A few rapid pops followed. Wanda saw the trails of lights fade, followed by tiny white-gold starbursts.

The muted sounds of whistles and clapping bounced off the buildings. Then another thunk-swish-boom.

Avery strutted on, but the brother twisted his neck back to watch. She grabbed his elbow. "You coming or not?"

He jerked it from her grip, his posture stiffening. The two strolled into the parking lot and headed toward the north end toward a cluster of parked vehicles.

Wanda scurried to enter as well but skirted along the edge of the curb, crouching low behind the tiny guard hut.

From her bent position, the hoods of the cars blocked the pair from her view. Drat.

Only one elm, planted in the center island, shaded the lot. The other trees all lined the fence like high school band marchers at attention. Not much cover. They'd spot her in a flash if she walked away from the cars.

Wanda trotted to the elm on tiptoe to get a better view. One loafer dislodged from her heel and she stumbled. But she caught herself with her palms. Ouch. Some asphalt gravel sliced into her hands. She wiped them on her slacks and ignored the stinging sensation.

Luckily, the siblings had not heard her. At least they gave no indication they did. They walked on and then stopped at a light-colored SUV.

Wanda took a chance and shuffled over to the nearest car. She peered over the back of the Honda's trunk, careful not to press her hands down less the pressure set off the alarm.

Nick knocked on the side of the van and a door slid open. He let his sister climb in first, then he followed. The door slid shut again.

What on earth?

Wanda waited. Then van's engine remained silent. No headlights emerged. Why?

Only one reason. They had arranged to meet someone. But who? Could it be Joe's gray SUV? Did his granddaughter, Alli, drive it?

More importantly, why would these three young people meet in a school parking lot? Drugs? No, she didn't want to think about that angle.

Had her gut been correct? Did these two grandkids have something to do with the burglaries after all? Did Alli mastermind it?

Wanda gritted her teeth. Or did her old nemesis somehow return undetected? Would she be that bold? Even more odd, would Aurora drive a soccer mom vehicle? Doubtful. Then who did they arrange to meet?

Curiosity drove her to move even closer. If she zigzagged between the small huddle of cars, maybe they'd not notice her. Wanda scanned for any shadows flanking the cars, made by the security lights' beams angled down from the roofs of the school buildings. They barely would cover her. In fact, except for that north corner where the SUV sat several spaces away from any other car, the place illuminated as bright as a front yard Christmas display.

She had to risk it. As quiet as possible, Wanda creeped, one foot in front of the other, bent at the waist. She heard a swoosh of more the fireworks overhead. In their illumination Wanda noticed the vehicle's color. Not gray. Not Joe's. More of a sandy tone.

Who drove that around town? Her mind flashed through streets she walked on a regular basis. Then it became too confusing to try and recall. Lots of the folks in town drove that sort of vehicle, especially since more and more young professionals with kids worked at home now so they'd moved here to escape the big city crime and traffic.

The side door opened. Nick crawled out. Then Avery emerged with a backpack slung over one shoulder.

A strong hand grasped Wanda's arm and dragged her backwards.

Another hand slammed across her mouth.

"Do. Not. Breathe. A. Word." A male voice hissed in her ear.

CHAPTER 40

Oh, no. Not again. Wanda had been kidnapped once before. That time, she'd persuaded them to let her go. No guarantee history could be repeated.

She shuffled her foot, felt a leg against her knee, raised her heel and jammed it into the assailant's shin. Okay, maybe wearing loafers with a strong sole had been a good idea.

A muffled curse word flew from the man's mouth followed by her name.

She knew that voice, and that aftershave. Jimmy Bob.

She wiggled from his grip and hissed in a low voice to avoid being heard over the cars. "Jimmy Bob? What on earth? You scared the bejeebers out of me."

The large officer rubbed his shin. "Sshh. Come with me."

She opened her mouth to tell him why she lurked in a

school parking lot but saw his eyes dash to the SUV. Ah, so that's why he'd arrived, too. Staking out the action.

She mouthed an okay.

He slowly opened the passenger door and motioned for her to get inside. She slid into the sedan and sat down. He must have switched off the button for the inside lights because it remained dark inside. Smart thinking. She noticed the side window had been lowered. She leaned out of it to view his face as he crouched down next to door.

"What's going on?"

"I've been surveilling them ever since the chief told me to. Checked their social media footprints. She is kinda wild. The brother, Nick, is two years younger and her puppy dog. They set off alarms in my mind. Especially when I discovered their mom had moved them to Cleburne six years ago to live with her ex's parents, thinking a smaller school and town might keep them out of trouble. Neither are doing well in college now, it appears."

Right. Changing the environment didn't always solve the problems. Not unless a strong sense of discipline followed. Sadly, the same temptations lurked in the hallways of any school nowadays.

The SUV's engine started up. It backed out, but without any headlights on, then turned and began to head out of the lot.

"Stay put." Jimmy Bob bolted from his hiding place with his revolver drawn. He stopped, legs straddled, gun aimed at the windshield. "HALT!"

The SUV screeched to a stop.

Avery started sprinting away from the scene, Nick followed close behind her.

"Oh, no you don't."

Wanda sprung from the passenger side of the sedan and ran as fast as she could. Two parking spaces from Avery, she bent low and let out a war cry as she increased her sprint then rammed the girl in the side.

They both tumbled to the ground, Wanda on top. Wanda slid the bag off stunned girl's shoulder to her forearm and maneuvered the other arm through the straps. Then she rocked back and pulled the bag as she twisted it, drawing both handles away from the girl's spine in a makeshift hold.

Avery screamed and wiggled but Wanda sat firmly on the girl's back side with both knees pressing into her hips.

Nick imitated a statue, feet stone-still to the asphalt. His mouth hung open.

Todd appeared out of nowhere. He cuffed Nick as Reagan relieved Wanda and secured Avery. In all the commotion, Wanda had not even noticed them arrive. Had they been parked close by, staking out the scene as well?

Reagan whispered, "Good job" to Wanda as she drew the pair away to a waiting squad car where the chief helped her lower them inside.

Then he climbed in the driver side while Reagan slid

into the front passenger side. They left, lights swirling, but no siren blaring.

Wanda knelt on the asphalt. Her heart's pounding drowned out the pops and booms of the fireworks finale illuminating the sky overhead. Her breaths huffed, making her lungs sting.

Her nephew stretched his hand out for Wanda to grab.

She nodded and took his offer, relying on his strength to draw her to her feet.

"You okay?" He scanned her face.

She bent to catch her breath and nodded. "And you?"

He remained silent.

When she raised her body, she saw his focus had shifted to the SUV.

Jimmy Bob had the driver sprawled face down across the hood, handcuffing her as he recited her legal rights. Dark hair fanned her face, but when he lifted her to her feet, Wanda saw who he'd arrested.

Rebecca?!

Todd didn't say a word, but his eyes followed as Jimmy Bob hauled his girlfriend toward the street that led to the police headquarters.

Rebecca never glanced in his direction. She jutted her chin as they passed.

Todd's jaw quivered then he ducked his head and kicked the asphalt with his boot.

Her nephew was not all right. Not at all.

CHAPTER 41

After Jimmy Bob and Rebecca walked through the gate onto 7th Street, Todd led Wanda to the sedan where she'd hidden with Jimmy Bob. He opened the door for her.

"Whose car is this?"

"Mine." His expression remained flat. "Rebecca talked me into getting it."

"When did you buy it?"

"Not now, Aunt Wanda, okay?" His voice cracked.

Poor guy. His heart must be shattering inside. She lowered her eyes and nodded.

They drove in silence the block to the police station's parking lot. Todd got out, opened her door, and then climbed the three steps to the employee door of the station. He held it open. She figured he meant for her to enter.

Something inside of her warned her that if they made eye contact, he might lose all control. She whispered her thanks and walked down the hallway. After all, by now she knew the way.

The bright lights assaulted her vision for a moment. She could hear Rebecca yelling at the top of her lungs, demanding an attorney. Poor, Todd. This must be ripping him apart.

Reagan saw Wanda and motioned her into the kitchen. "Can you make some coffee? I stink at it. Make a full pot. It's gonna be a long night."

Glad to have something to do, Wanda agreed. While the machine gurgled and spewed, she glanced down the hall. Avery and Nick sat on the bench, their hands still cuffed. Reagan went back to stand next to them with a clipboard. They seemed to be talking a little, and she wrote down every word.

Todd stationed himself off to the side, his hand visibly on his revolver holster. The boy, Nick, glanced in Todd's direction. The color left his cheeks. What was that about?

Rebecca's voice still echoed from the examination room, but it had less volume. Then Wanda overheard the chief speaking to her. In a moment he opened the door. "You'll get your phone call, Miss Epson. Hang tight."

Wanda ducked back into the kitchen and began separating Styrofoam cups. She heard the chief's boot clunk against the linoleum floor then scuffle to a stop. "Coffee. Good. I could use some."

She smiled. "Almost brewed."

He came over and rested his hip against the counter. "Exactly what were you doing at the school?"

Oh, boy. Here we go. "Following Avery and Nick."

"Because?"

"Call it women's intuition. Something seemed, I don't know . . . off." She forced a laugh. "Little did I know I'd run headlong into a stake out. Sorry."

"Yeah, well, you came very close to blowing the whole thing. I could arrest you as well, you know, for impeding justice."

"Todd's been through enough, don't you think?" She raised her chin and stared him down.

The chief stared back, then a sad grin inched one side of his mouth. He took a cup, poured his coffee, and left without saying another word.

Wanda finally took a breath. She made herself a cup of coffee, adding real sugar and milk to the brew. No one had told her to stay but they hadn't told her to leave. Call it motherly instinct, but she wanted to hover close by in case Todd wanted to talk.

It reminded her of the times he came home from high school with a sullen expression but when she asked him what was wrong, he muttered the one word all teenagers know—nothing. Just as her two kids had done.

Eventually, in his own time, he'd find her and decide to spill whatever huddled in his heart. He would this time as well. She only needed to be patient. *Yes, Lord, I'm learning.*

The wall clock read a few minutes before ten. DiAne would be sawing wood by now, but Wanda felt a responsibility to let her know what had happened. Betty Sue and Ev, too. May as well try the conference call app that came with her phone's update.

She called Betty Sue, then when she answered hit the call for Evelyn, merged it, and then did the same for DiAne. "Well, ladies I'm at the police station, but no worries. The culprits have been apprehended. The case solved."

All three started chatting at once. Wanda hushed them and closed the kitchen door. Quietly she explained the whole thing to them.

"Rebecca? Todd's Rebecca?" Betty Sue clucked her tongue.

"She isn't his anymore." Wanda sighed. "I am not sure how involved she is but she appears to be the ringleader."

"Why?" Evelyn's voice squeaked.

"I haven't a clue. They are all being processed right now. I'm lying low in the kitchen." Wanda took a sip of coffee. "Just wanted to fill you three in. DiAne, I may be a while."

"Of course. Take care. I'm fine."

"I hope they have your jewelry. I feel so bad it was stolen from my house."

"I hope they have it, too, Wanda. But if not, my insurance company investigators will help track the pieces down." She paused. "They are just baubles. Todd is more important. Give him my love."

Betty Sue and Evelyn echoed with an amen. Then Evelyn led them in a short prayer before disconnecting.

Wanda's heart warmed and she silently thanked God for her dear friends.

Julie B Cosgrove

CHAPTER 42

The police kitchen cupboard lay pretty bare, the drawers filled with mainly takeout packets of ketchup and the like. But she found some sandwich cookies and a sleeve of saltine crackers. Inside the fridge she saw a block of cheddar cheese. It took a while wielding a plastic knife but she managed to cut the cheese into square slices and placed them on the crackers to nuke for 15 seconds in the microwave. She arranged the cookies on another plate and set both snacks on the table.

As if by osmosis, Jimmy Bob and Todd entered.

"Yum. I'm starved." Jimmy Bob placed two crackers with cheese and three cookies on a paper napkin and headed back to the hall. Todd stared at the table, then up at her.

"You still here?"

"Thought I'd make myself useful. I figured eventually

one of you would want to take my statement."

He scratched his brow "Yeah."

Then he pulled out a chair and sat.

Wanda waited.

The clock ticked.

The coffee pot hissed.

Todd glared at the cheese. He blinked and let out a deep sigh.

Wanda swallowed hard and laid her hand on his.

He glanced at it and laid his other hand on top then patted her fingers. "This is tough."

"I can only imagine."

He released his grip and sat back, his eyes traveling to the ceiling tiles. "I really liked her. Or perhaps I liked the idea of her liking me. A lot. I mean in high school she had been way out of my league."

"I remember."

"We really had fun together this past year or so, you know? And she kept coming to visit Vicki in her pregnancy but then to see me as well. Then she told me she'd be babysitting the Rollin's house so we could spend more time together. *Then* she got the job at the elementary school and wanted to rent a two-bedroom apartment across from me. Said when my lease came due in August, I could move in with her instead. It started getting a bit weird."

He rocked forward and grabbed Wanda's hand again. "Over the past month, Rebecca became very clingy.

Hinting for a ring. Constantly mentioning how happy Mason and Vicki were and how much a baby would make their lives complete. It began to freak me out."

"I bet." She knew if she kept her comments short, he'd keep talking.

"She hated you, Aunt Wanda. She felt we were too close. That our relationship bordered on abnormal. Her parents had always been distant, involved in their volunteer duties, and occupations. At first, I figured she had a jealousy streak toward you, but it became more sinister than that. I finally realized she wanted to drive you out of town so she could have me all to herself."

"Oh, Todd. I am sorry. When did you find out?"

"I guess when you described the burglar in more detail it clicked. Maybe I had refused to put it all together before then. I walked and walked and as I did the pieces began to merge. In the meantime, Jimmy Bob tailed the kids and saw them get into her SUV. He texted me. Slowly, the picture took shape."

"How did they get involved?"

"Their other grandparents lived next door to Rebecca in the same condo community in Cleburne. Rebecca met Avery last summer by the pool. She said Nick could hack into anything, even cell phones. When DiAne mentioned that might be how the burglar knew about the word puzzle clues, it clicked in my brain."

"I see." Wanda let out a small sigh. The pain in his

face broke her heart.

"They were the ones that rigged your oven and hung the tennis shoes up with the sign. The same muddy pair you saw on the back patio. Jimmy Bob confirmed it."

"I figured as much. Maybe that is why I tailed them tonight."

He glanced at her and nodded. "You always were intuitive."

"Todd, I have to ask. What about all the money? The jewelry?"

Todd almost smiled. "When we searched the SUV, we found both DiAne's and Beverly's jewelry and most of the money in the spare tire well. Not sure what Rebecca expected to do with it. Maybe she didn't either. This had to do with ruining you, not making her wealthy."

"Thank goodness the jewelry was there." She sighed in relief for both DiAne and Beverly. "But the money? Most of it?"

"The kids had the rest of the cash on them. She'd just paid them off."

"So, none of the merchants have suffered a loss?"

"Well, except for Ray. But his insurance is covering the damages to his restaurant. And Jay is handling the damage to Anna's Antique's backdoor."

Reagan slipped into the kitchen. She sat down, grabbed a cookie, and shoved it in her mouth. Then she turned to Todd. "Avery had the money Rebecca paid them in her backpack. Once we pulled it out, Nick and Avery sang like mockingbirds, right, Todd."

He examined his thumbnail. "Yep."

"They are in cell two. By the way, their mom, the attorney, is heading here."

"Wonderful. This should be fun. A legal beagle and mother hen rolled into one." He chuckled, but the tone bordered on pathetic.

Wanda blinked back tears. Her heart ached for him as he went over the protocol with Reagan so she'd be better prepared when the mother arrived. This had to be so tough on him.

Then she noticed Reagan's face. Sympathy lay in her expression as well, but Wanda detected something deeper in her eyes as they landed on Todd's face and remained there. She even scooted a bit closer and tilted her head as if . . .

Could it be? Reagan had a sweet face and a nice figure. She was polite, always cleanly dressed. She went to church. Obviously had ethics and morals.

And she did seem to hang on Todd's every word.

Acknowledgements

I want to thank my son, James. If I have a muse, it is him, I guess. Though he is not in law enforcement, I thought of him as I have developed Todd through this series.

I owe my thanks to three other people, who have graciously allowed me to use their names in this book. Anne Graves, my sister, who always supports my writing and buys my books even though she is not an avid reader. To DiAne Gates, a great Christian author in her own right, whom I have known for years. No matter your age, you should read her books for young adults and children. They are marvelous. Finally, to her friend, Patricia Farmer in Jacksonville, Florida, where I used to live. Though we never met, I feel a bond with her and appreciate that she reads everything I write.

Of course, I owe a huge amount of gratitude to Marji Laine at Write Integrity Press and her staff, especially editor Shirley Crowder. I am so blessed to be contracted as an author with this publishing company. They are wonderful to work with and so very supportive of their writers.

I write all my mysteries with a message. The one takeaway I hope you, the reader, receives is that human love can never be totally satisfying, nor can it fulfill all of your needs. People are fickle. Anger and jealousy can easily emerge and cloud emotions. If we depend on the approval of others as our motivation or measure of self-worth, we will inevitably get our feelings bruised.

Only the eternal, unchangeable, all merciful, and constant love of God is truly unconditional. It is why He hung on the cross to take on our sins. We are so precious in His sight and His love for us is beyond comparison. He may not like some of the things we do, but His love for us never diminishes.

However, when bound together in His love, we humans can become precious gifts to each other. That is something we should nurture and cherish at all costs.

May He bless you and keep you in His grace,

About the Author

Whodunnit? My mom used to ask us that with a hand cocked on her hip, peering into our wide-eyed faces. Naturally the blame trickled down to the youngest one—me. I had to solve the crime so I could plead my innocence.

On walks through the Texas Hill Country with my dad, I became a keen observer of nature, and later in life as an adult and writer, of human nature. So sleuthing is part of my DNA.

I wrote award-winning works in high school creative writing class, but then life edged in. Even so, on my long commutes I'd make up storylines in my head. After my husband passed away, the desire to write returned. My sister suggested I write mysteries, which had long been my favorite genre.

Now I absorb mysteries whenever I get the chance then let the whodunnits capture my imagination, and my keyboard. I think I'm finally becoming who God intended me to be.

Besides writing mystery, suspense-romance, and short

stories, I am an editor for two Christian publishing companies as well as a freelance editor. For the past twelve years, I have regularly written for several devotional publications. My own blog, *Where Did You Find God Today*, has readers in over 50 countries. Visit my website at www.juliebcosgrove.com

Julie B Cosgrove

Mystery and Suspense by Write Integrity Press

Thank you
for reading our books!

Please consider leaving a review for the author
on the purchase page for this book.

Look for other books
published by

P

Pursued Books
an imprint of

W

Write Integrity Press
www.WriteIntegrity.com

www.ingramcontent.com/pod-product-compliance
Lightning Source LLC
Chambersburg PA
CBHW070555260626
47161CB00002B/610